Joyce Moyer Hostetter

AIM

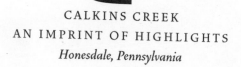
CALKINS CREEK
AN IMPRINT OF HIGHLIGHTS
Honesdale, Pennsylvania

Calkins Creek
An Imprint of Highlights
815 Church Street
Honesdale, Pennsylvania 18431
calkinscreekbooks.com
Printed in China

ISBN: 978-1-62979-673-4 (hc) • 978-1-68437-276-8 (pb)
978-1-62979-746-5 (eBook)
Library of Congress Control Number: 2016932209

First paperback edition, 2019
10 9 8 7 6 5 4 3 2 1

Design by Barbara Grzeslo
The text of this book is set in Sabon.

For Carolyn Yoder,
who suggested I find a story in my own backyard,
which, as it turns out, is the very best place for a series
to begin

PROLOGUE

It was Pop who taught me to shoot.
He showed me how to aim and hold that
    gun real steady.

But when it came to life,
aiming wasn't so easy for him.
Seemed like he was always stumbling
    around
looking for something that would make
    him happy.
I don't reckon he ever found it.
When he died,
I was stuck with Granddaddy and with
    stories
of how, back during the Great War,
he turned my pop into his own personal
    enemy.
Pop was just a boy then.

The way I figure it,
what I learned from the two of them
and from my own dumb mistakes
is enough to fill a book.

1

POP AND ME
July 1941

"Hand me that wrench." Pop wiggled his grease-covered fingers.

I gave it to him, but I wanted real bad to get my hands on his repair job. "I could do that if I had me half a chance," I said.

"Too bad," said Pop. "I'm not taking half a chance on messing up Miss Pauline's car." Pop had been in a growly mood ever since Granddaddy moved in last week. But it wouldn't make a difference if he was in a good mood. Fixing cars was his job. My part was handing him tools and fetching him cups of cold well water when he was thirsty.

Sometimes I wondered if I'd ever get to show him what I could do.

Just then my hound dogs started howling. "Hush, Jesse. Be quiet, Butch." I squatted and scratched Jesse behind his ear. "Pop, it's the Honeycutts—in a truck!"

"Leroy don't have a truck."

"He's driving one now. A '35 Chevrolet."

The Honeycutts' oldest girl, Ann Fay, was hanging out the truck window. "Hey, Junior," she hollered. "Look what we got!" Leroy parked right beside us under the big oak tree where Pop fixed cars.

Pop leaned in close so only I could hear. "Sounds to me like a box of rocks." Then he called out, "Howdy, neighbor. Where'd you find that dandy?"

Leroy hopped out of the truck and pointed to the name on the door.

Hutton and Bourbonnais Lumber Company
Hickory, North Carolina

He grinned. "The boss called it a rust bucket. Said it used too much oil, so he replaced it with a brand-new one. Of course, this is coming out of my wages."

Pop didn't own a truck or a car, so I expected him to turn green as moss right in front of Leroy. But he took it like a man. "I'm right proud for you, Leroy. Mind if I take a look?" Pop lifted the hood of the truck and reached for the dipstick. He pulled it out, wiped it clean with a rag, and put it back in. Then he pulled it out again. "Oil looks okay now," he said. "But keep an eye on it or you'll be rebuilding the engine for sure." He pointed to the pulleys hanging from the big oak tree overhead. "My block and tackle is just waiting."

Leroy nodded. "It could use a tune-up. Think you could help me?"

Ann Fay climbed out and grabbed her daddy's arm. "Can I help?" She was only ten years old, but I declare, she was like a pint-sized Leroy with her black hair and those blue eyes. All she needed was a pair of overalls to finish her off.

People said me and Pop looked alike too. Same stocky build and brown hair that wanted to curl whether we liked it or not. But we didn't go together like biscuits and gravy the way Ann Fay and Leroy did. Seemed like when I turned eleven years old, me and Pop went from being biscuits and gravy to vinegar and baking soda. When you put the two of us together, there was bound to be some fizzing going on.

Jesse came sniffing at Ann Fay's feet, so she scooped him up and snuggled into him like he was Bobby, her baby brother. "Hey, cutie pie. I sure wish I had a dog like you."

She just wanted a dog and I just wanted that truck. I walked all around it. There were a few rust spots and a dent in the fender. But it had a nice blue color. I was already scheming how I could get Leroy to let me drive it. I walked over to the driver's door and stepped onto the running board.

"Go on," said Leroy. "Hop in."

So I did. Ann Fay climbed into the passenger side.

"Someday *I'll* have a car," I said. "Except I want one of those 1940 Studebakers with a cargo box that fits in the back. That would be like having a car and a truck, all in one."

Ann Fay probably didn't know what a cargo box was, and evidently she didn't care either. "Can you believe it, Junior? My daddy has got his very own truck. We won't be hitching rides with the Hinkle sisters or Peggy Sue's family anymore. Take me for a ride, Junior."

I shook my head. "First I gotta learn to drive. And Lord knows when that'll happen. Pop ain't been willing to let me try."

Leroy came to the driver's door, so I hopped out and watched while he got in and turned the truck around. Before he could leave, Ann Fay called me to her window. "Here's the paper," she said. "Almost forgot to give it to you." She shoved a copy of the *Hickory Daily Record* into my hands.

The Honeycutts almost always passed the paper on to us. The only reason they had one in the first place was because the Hinkle sisters let them read their copy when they were done with it.

I unfolded the paper. First thing that caught my eye was a warning from President Roosevelt saying that Americans should be willing to pledge our lives to preserve freedom.

In other words, he was preparing us to go to war. So far, my pop and Leroy didn't have to register with the army because they were over twenty-eight years old. *And* they had families. But if America joined the war against Adolf Hitler, there was a chance they'd have to serve. And according to most people, it wasn't a matter of *if* we joined the war; it was a matter of *when*.

The Germans had already taken over Poland and France and a bunch of other countries. They'd tried to take England but couldn't, and now they were marching through Russia, fighting their way to the capital. Besides all that, they had submarines in the Atlantic Ocean, attacking whoever they took a notion to.

But I didn't want to think just then about war and Pop being called up and maybe even getting killed. I flipped over to the sports page for a quick look at the report on Joe DiMaggio's hitting streak. He was up to forty-seven games now, and it looked like he couldn't be stopped.

I put the paper on a crate sitting in the yard and went back to help Pop with Miss Pauline's carburetor. "Can I finish adjusting that?"

"No." He didn't even lift his head to look at me. "This is my mechanic shop. Find your own job." He kept right on working. Finally he said, as if he'd grabbed the idea right out of thin air, "Your pal Calvin quit school. You can too."

Calvin Settlemyre. Pop and I went night-fishing on the river with him and his daddy. Used to, anyway—but not lately. It seemed like the more Pop took to drinking whiskey, the more certain people kept their distance. After all, his ways might rub off on them. For all they knew, I could be a bad apple too.

But if there was anything I wanted, it was to show the world that the Bledsoes could be as upstanding as anybody else. "I'm going to high school, Pop," I said. "Momma wants me to. And I finally made it to ninth grade."

"Yeah, well, you go on, then. After the first day, quit. Least you can say you went to high school." Pop laughed and poked me in the chest with his wrench.

I laughed too, but not for real. It was just an act-like-it-didn't-hurt laugh. A go-along-with-Pop laugh. "But Pop, I can play baseball this year."

He snorted. "There's only one Joe DiMaggio. And one of these days his streak will end just like that." Pop snapped his fingers in front of my eyeballs.

"Yeah," I said. "But that don't stop him from playing."

"Nope," he said. "But I can stop you."

He stuck out his hand, and I put a screwdriver in it. It was time to adjust the carburetor.

"Start 'er up," he said. "And cover the seat so you don't get it dirty. I won't have you disgracing me in front of the neighbors."

"Yes, sir." The car belonged to the Hinkle sisters just up the road. They were proper ladies, especially Miss Pauline. I spread a clean feed sack across the seat, then slid behind the steering wheel, pushed the starter button, and turned the key. I felt like revving that engine high as it would go, but I knew better.

Pop poked his head up past the hood and hollered. "Let it idle." He tinkered with the screws on the carburetor and hollered again. "Now rev it up. Hold her steady. Whoa, not so much."

We went back and forth like that, him hollering instructions and me trying to get it just right. In my mind's eye I could see exactly what his hands were doing because more than once I'd watched him work on Wayne Walker's 1940 Ford, with Wayne giving it the gas and Pop adjusting the screws.

When Pop was satisfied with the sound of things, he put the air filter back on and closed the hood. I stuck my head out the window. "How about I ride along when you take it back?"

"How about you see if your momma has supper ready? It won't take me a minute to run this up the road."

Miss Pauline's '35 Plymouth sat there purring like a cat on a Sunday afternoon and Pop wouldn't even let me ride with him. If you asked me, I deserved a little something for being his flunky.

Pop scrubbed the grease off his hands with kerosene, then went to the back porch to wash with soap and water. He lathered up his arms, singing "Amazing Grace" and how it saved a wretch like him.

He sure could act like a wretch.

I closed my eyes for a minute, pretending I was on the highway driving away from Pop. To some place where I could get me a little respect.

"Time to stop daydreaming." Pop was back.

"Yes, sir." I slid out from under the wheel.

"I meant what I said about school. Find yourself a job and take care of your momma." He climbed in the car. "I'll be back before you can say 'Yankee Doodle Dandy.'" Then he drove off and left me to put the tools away.

"Yankee Doodle Dandy," I said. And he wasn't even out of the driveway yet.

2

GRANDDADDY
July 1941

Momma used the skirt of her apron to dab at the sweat on her round face. "Junior, dish up a bowl of beans for Hammer."

I crumbled cornbread into the beans. And added raw onions. Granddaddy would yell if I didn't. When I carried the bowl into the bedroom, he was sleeping in his rocking chair with his radio on. They were saying something about German U-boats sinking British ships and wondering how long it would be until those submarines attacked the United States.

Granddaddy's gray hair was flat on one side from sleeping on it. I nudged his leg with my knee. "I brung your supper."

"Thunderation! You fool. You woke me up." His eyelids slid shut again, and his mouth fell open like a trapdoor without a hook. A dried stream of tobacco snuff ran from the corner of his mouth and down onto his neck.

"Wake up. They're talking about America joining the war again."

That got him going. "Huh!" he grumbled. "That yellow-bellied president is too chicken to take us to war. He ain't half the man the Colonel was."

The Colonel—that was Theodore Roosevelt, who evidently loved war. But he'd been dead for twenty-some years. So far, our president, Franklin Roosevelt, had steered clear of fighting, and I figured he was doing his best for the good of the country.

I turned the radio up so Granddaddy would listen and maybe even eat supper. He reached for the bowl, and I turned to go. But his voice chased after me. "With any luck, they'll call up your pop and turn him into a real man."

It seemed like he couldn't wait for Pop to be drafted. Or dead.

Granddaddy had been living with us for a week, but it didn't take one meal to figure out that he and Pop couldn't eat supper at the same table. After the first day, Momma started carrying Granddaddy's food into the bedroom to keep the two of them apart. But Pop and Granddaddy could argue without being in the same room. Pop would come in the house singing *"Ain't gonna study war no more"*—just to get Granddaddy going— and the next thing we knew, Granddaddy's radio would be turned up loud as possible. Then Pop would march over to the bedroom door and pull it shut. Hard.

I wanted to ask Pop why he hated his daddy so much, but talking about Granddaddy might set him off and I didn't plan to be the cause of him going out drinking with Wayne Walker.

Back in the kitchen, Momma had three plates dished up, but Pop still wasn't home. "I bet Miss Pauline got to talking," I said.

"No," said Momma. "It's her suppertime and she won't let anyone interfere with her schedule. You know that, Junior."

"Maybe Miss Dinah, then."

"Pauline keeps Dinah on schedule too," said Momma.

Miss Pauline was a schoolteacher who liked doing things just so. As a matter of fact, she taught ninth grade. I sure wished there was a way to miss having her for my teacher this year. Besides quitting school, that is.

Momma sighed and glanced out the window. "Let's eat."

While I was still eating, Granddaddy hollered for me to come into his room—which was actually *my* room, with him added into it.

"I'll be there when I'm done eating, Granddaddy."

I finished up and found him on the floor, dragging a pasteboard box out from under the bed. "Open that," he said. "We're gonna fancy up these walls." Granddaddy had only a left hand. There was a scarred-up stub at the end of his right arm—something to do with a mill accident.

First thing out of the box was a studio portrait of a soldier. "That's your great-granddaddy there."

"Your daddy?"

"Yup. Gideon Bledsoe. Confederate Army." Granddaddy picked up the tin can he kept by the rocker, spit a stream of tobacco juice into the can, and kept on talking. "He was a pipsqueak when he joined. By the time he came back, he was hard as nails. I wasn't born yet, but I can attest to the truth of it. A war will grow you right up."

Gideon looked to be about my age. Fourteen. His eyes were might near as shiny as the buttons on his uniform. His dark hair curled out from under his wool cap. Looking at that picture, I couldn't deny him for a relative of mine. He held his gun across his chest like that was the thing he wanted most to show off in the picture. As if the gun was what made his eyes sparkle the way they did.

"Set that on the bureau. And we're gonna need some tacks."

Lucky for Granddaddy, Momma had some tacks in an old baking powder can. When I came back with them, Granddaddy unfolded a Theodore Roosevelt campaign poster and I tacked it up, like he told me to, on the wall above the iron bedframe. Then he started pulling newspaper pictures out of his box—local boys who were serving in the armed forces right that minute.

"Those fellas are fighting for your freedom. You better appreciate it, too."

"Yes, Granddaddy. I sure do."

Granddaddy started telling me which of those soldiers were from Brookford, the small mill town where he raised Pop. My aunts lived there. Brookford was only a few miles away, but a body would hardly know it, considering how the family never saw each other. Pop could ride past his sisters' houses without flicking an eyelash.

I didn't pay much attention to Granddaddy talking about the Brookford boys because my eyes kept wandering to that picture of Gideon Bledsoe. He looked so young. What was it like to fight in something so awful as the Civil War?

"Junior." Momma was calling. "You're gonna have to do the milking." That meant she'd given up on Pop.

"Yeah, Pop," I grumbled. "Reason I can't play baseball is I gotta fill in for you when you take a notion to go out and get drunk." I took the milk bucket and headed for the barn. While I was out there, it started to rain. The sound of it on the roof set up a rhythm for the milking. Afterward, I leaned into Pop's mule and stroked his mane. "Grover," I said, "it appears he's out drinking again. Momma's gonna be downhearted. Don't it make you mad?"

When I went back into my room, Granddaddy was

getting off the chamber pot and pulling up his britches. "Left you a little something to carry out," he said.

I sure didn't want to be dumping his dooky, but I couldn't sleep with that smell in the room either. "Granddaddy," I said. "That pot is for using in the middle of the night. We have an outhouse for the rest of the time."

"Hmph. It's raining out there. Besides, I'm too old to be trotting to a johnny house."

Granddaddy wasn't that old. Not even sixty, according to Momma. His legs worked just fine. But he thought he was too good for country living.

I emptied the pot because, after all, what choice did I have? "Pop," I said, talking to myself mostly, "I don't much like your daddy either."

After washing on the back porch, I pulled up a stool and stayed out there, listening to the steady clattering of rain on the porch roof. It crossed my mind to bring my blankets and pillow out there and let the rhythm of it put me to sleep.

Seemed like it had rained the whole month of July. Pop's garden had so much corn he declared he could feed the state of North Carolina. He'd sold it by the dozen out along the highway. And more than likely a couple of bushels went to Wayne Walker for making whiskey.

The two of them were probably together right this minute.

Finally I headed for bed. But for me, bed wasn't

exactly a bed. Not since Granddaddy arrived. My bed was big enough for two people, but after three nights of him snoring and farting, I decided I'd rather sleep on the floor. So I'd piled me up a few featherbeds and grabbed my pillow and moved to the corner.

It was up into the night and I was sound asleep when Butch and Jesse started howling from under the front porch. Someone banged on the door, so I got up and went to be with Momma, just in case it wasn't Pop—or even if it was. Midnight surprises never seemed to turn out for the good. And this time it was the deputy sheriff, standing there with water dripping off the brim of his hat.

3

BAD NEWS
July 1941

The policeman leaned in and spoke up extra loud, but the rain on the roof still almost drowned him out. "Mrs. Bledsoe?"

"Yes." Momma's voice was a whisper, but I could see the words on her lips. "What's wrong?"

"Could I come inside, please?"

She stood there not moving. I knew she wanted to shut that door in his face and pretend her husband was in bed where he belonged at this hour of the night.

"Yes, sir," I said. "Come on in."

Momma sat in the closest chair—on the edge of it, like she didn't plan to stay long. I could tell she just wanted that deputy to say what he'd come for and then leave. He stood by the door and let the water drip onto the rag rug she'd braided.

He stuttered around for a minute or two and finally started to walk the floor, stopping in front of the mantelpiece. He picked up the framed photograph of Momma and Pop on the day they got married. Was he trying to figure out if that skinny lady in the picture was the same person as the heavyset woman waiting for him to speak? Maybe he thought he was in the wrong house. I sure *hoped* he was, because him being there had to mean something bad.

Finally he put the picture down and turned to face us.

"I'm sorry, Mrs. Bledsoe," he said. "We found Axel over on Hog Hill by the side of the road. Ma'am, we need you to come and identify the body."

The body? What did he mean by that?

But Momma knew exactly what the officer was saying. "He can't be dead." Her voice wobbled and cracked. "He was just here. He wasn't sick. He's never sick." Which was a strange thing for her to be saying, considering how many times she'd told people he was taken ill. What she really meant was that he'd passed out from too much bootleg whiskey.

All of a sudden I felt light in the head—like *I* was fixing to pass out. But I had to be close to Momma, so I sat on the arm of her chair and she sagged up against me. I put my arm around her shoulder and we sat there, quivering. She was twisting the hem of her chenille bed jacket and picking at its fluffs. Staring at it real steady, as if ignoring the policeman would mean he wasn't even there.

I heard Momma swallow, and I heard the scratchy sound of her fingers on her bed jacket.

The deputy cleared his throat and shuffled his feet.

"We better go now, Momma. He needs us to identify the body." I couldn't believe I'd said that. The body. As if Pop wasn't a person, even.

Later, when I saw him there on the table with a sheet pulled over him and his feet sticking out, I knew it was him by his shoes. Brown wingtips with a hole in each sole. Red clay caked to the edges.

But Momma wanted to see his face. She sat there for a long time, pulling bits of grass from his thick brown hair and holding his hand—which they hadn't done a spanking good job of cleaning up. There was some mud under his fingernails. So I fished his knife out of his pocket for her. She used the edge of that blade to clean under every single nail.

I didn't want to see how gentle she was, as if she thought that blade could hurt him. And I sure didn't want to cry. I just wanted her to stop so the deputy could take us home. I wanted to crawl between my blankets and listen to the rain pounding on the roof and pretend that none of this had ever happened. "Momma," I said, "the undertaker will clean him up proper. He'll look real nice. You wait and see."

But she didn't pay me no mind. She just whispered his name. "Axel Bledsoe. Have mercy, Axel. What have you done to yourself?"

The officer said it seemed to be a normal death. No marks on the body. No foul play.

Finally, after the coroner promised her she could see

Pop again before the burying, the deputy convinced her to go home.

He drove real careful because the windshield wipers slowed down every time he stepped on the gas. Water gurgled against the windows. It beat on the roof and swished under the tires, making a racket that bumped into my thoughts.

Pop is dead. Pop is dead. The words bounced around, looking for a place to land in my mind.

I heard other things—the crunch of leaves under our feet while Pop and me headed into the woods with our guns, Momma begging him to give up drinking, the sound of him coming in the door late at night, singing "*Let me call you sweetheart.*"

For some reason, that was his stumbling-in-drunk song. I came close to hating him on those nights. Here he'd just done the thing Momma despised most, drunk himself senseless and acted the fool, for Lord only knows *who* to see. Why did he think he could sing his way back into her good graces?

Momma deserved better than that. If there was anything she wanted, it was to have a man who was as upstanding as her daddy was. Momma came from good people who worked hard for a living and held their heads high when they went out in public. Only thing was, her family lived in China Grove, and she didn't see them much. Maybe she would have, if Pop was different, but they didn't have much use for him.

Back home, I told Granddaddy that Pop had died. It was the wee hours of the morning when I came in, and I knew he was awake on account of the grunting sounds he was making. "Axel's dead," I told him. The grunting stopped. All I could hear was rain on the roof. "They found him by the side of the road. But he wasn't hit by a car or nothing like that."

It was quiet for a long time and then Granddaddy spoke up. "The Yankees won," he said. "DiMaggio got two hits." Next thing I knew, he was snoring and I was on the floor wide awake with a childish song running through my head. *It's raining, it's pouring, the old man is snoring.*

He didn't even care.

Maybe the two of them really couldn't live in the same house and Pop just let Granddaddy crowd him out. Was it possible for a person to choose when to die? Was that what Pop had done?

I felt like crying. Maybe it was because Granddaddy didn't act the least bit sad that Pop was gone. What would that be like—to die and not have your own father give a hoot?

I could've cried for myself, too. It wasn't like me and Pop were connected the way Ann Fay and Leroy were. But I always wanted us to be. Mostly, I wanted the kind of family they had. Leroy carried his lunch bucket off to work every day and came home at the end of the week with real wages that his family could count on.

26

I never had any reason for believing such a thing could happen to us, but that hadn't stopped me from dreaming. I kept hoping Pop would turn himself around and become the kind of man that people didn't whisper about behind his back. Now I knew for sure it would never happen. As a matter of fact, he'd just given them one more thing to shake their heads over and pity me and Momma for.

When I pulled the pillow over my head and stuffed my face into my featherbed, I wasn't crying for what me and Momma had just lost. I cried for what we never had in the first place.

4

FUNERAL
July 1941

His heart gave out. That's what we told everybody. And it was true. But I could tell from the looks on people's faces that they knew there was more to the story. I went to the Hinkle sisters' house and called Momma's people in China Grove so they would know that Pop was gone. When they showed up—Uncle Tag and Granny and Gramps and the rest of them—they kept asking questions about his whereabouts that night.

We didn't have any answers about what he did after he took the Hinkle sisters' car back. He must've hitched a ride to Peewee Hudson's sweet potato house on Hog Hill. There was sure to be card playing and drinking going on in the back room.

But why did Pop start out walking toward home? That's what I wanted to know. Pop didn't mind a light rain, but it wasn't like him to walk the roads in a downpour. And couldn't he have caught a ride with somebody?

In his funeral sermon, Reverend Price told everybody how Pop was a regular church attender—except when he was sick. Momma twitched when he said that. She was probably thinking about all those times she shook the reverend's hand on the way out of church and explained to him that Pop was not feeling well. Again.

Beside me, Uncle Tag cleared his throat. I knew exactly what he was thinking. My mind went back to the day I turned eleven years old. Momma had cooked a big birthday dinner and invited the neighbors and her relatives. Pop had made a table from boards laid across sawbucks. But he climbed onto Grover and rode off, saying he had a surprise to pick up for me. He didn't come back in time for dinner. So, finally, after it was already cold, Momma started without him.

Eventually he came. We heard him before we saw him. He was singing "Happy Birthday," but the words sounded slow and mushy. When he climbed down from Grover he landed on his backside. I think everybody gasped or let out some kind of holler. That's how I remember it anyway, like a chorus of worry that gushed out of them. Leroy ran to him, and with his help, Pop staggered into the house, singing *Happy birthday, dear Junior.* In that mushy voice.

I still remember Momma standing there with both hands over her mouth, tears splashing onto her fingers and running down her arms. It was the first time either of us saw Pop drunk. But there were many more. Somehow, I knew it had something to do with my birthday. It was my fault. It had to be.

The coroner said that Pop's death was the result of his heavy drinking. But the reverend didn't mention a word about Pop's drinking habit. "Axel Bledsoe had a heart as big as Bakers Mountain," he said. A whole bunch of *amen*s rose up out of the congregation. All of a sudden Pop had turned into a saint instead of someone the deacons were constantly trying to pull back onto the straight and narrow. I saw Peggy Sue Rhinehart's mother dabbing at her eyes. Even Momma's family was acting weepy. But maybe they were all just worried about her.

Momma herself didn't cry once during the funeral. And it wasn't because she didn't care. I knew how she hankered after him when he wasn't home and how she fixed him pecan pies because they were his favorite.

I didn't cry either, but I cared. Of course I did. He was my pop, even if other people wouldn't want him for theirs. After all the hunting in the woods and fixing cars under the oak tree, how could he just die and not be there anymore?

When the service was over, we followed the coffin down the aisle. There, at the last pew, was one of Pop's sisters, waiting for us. Aunt Lucille took Momma's arm and walked with us out of the church. She was headed toward the graveyard too, until her heels started sinking into the soft ground. Then she stopped. "I can't stay," she said. "But I wanted to pay my respects and tell you how sorry I am."

Momma nodded. "Will you be by to see your daddy?"

Aunt Lucille looked off toward the trees behind the graveyard. "It figures—he couldn't come to his own son's funeral. No, I have to get back to my family."

"Where's Lillian?"

Aunt Lucille shrugged her broad shoulders. "Am I my sister's keeper?"

Momma let out a big sigh. "I guess not. But what about Hammer? We'll need help with him, now that Axel's gone."

You would think, from the way Aunt Lucille turned and walked away, that Momma hadn't just mentioned Granddaddy. It was like all of a sudden Lucille was deaf as a dipstick. She hurried back to Uncle James's 1936 Ford. I noticed James was in the driver's seat, waiting on her. And my cousins were climbing in a tree in the churchyard. It seemed like someone had to die for me to realize Pop had a family. And even then I could barely tell. Who knew if we'd ever see them again?

After Pop was in the ground, people came up to Momma and bragged on him. "Axel helped me bring the hay in before that first big rain," said Garland Abernethy.

Jerry Jones took Momma's hand. "Axel fixed the brakes on my truck. And he didn't charge me one red cent."

"No, of course not," said Momma. "He wouldn't."

She was right. Pop was bighearted that way. But wouldn't it have been neighborly for Jerry to offer a red cent or two? Didn't he think our family needed to pay bills? At least, when Pop worked for Garland, he'd get paid in hay or animal feed.

My old fishing buddy Calvin Settlemyre dragged himself over to the graveside. I could tell from the hang of his head that he didn't want to be there. "It's real sad about your pop," he said.

As if I didn't know that already. I just nodded. "Thanks for coming."

He turned away then and went back to the other boys our age who were catching some shade under a maple tree. It seemed like they'd decided to let him do the talking. A couple of them glanced in my direction but turned away when they saw me looking.

It didn't matter that much. They were mostly my Sunday-morning pals. Calvin was the only one of them I saw outside of church and school. And who knew if Ralph Settlemyre would ever take me fishing with him and Calvin again?

Myrtle Honeycutt stepped up then. "Bessie, we want you and Junior to come over for supper, if you will. Miss Pauline and Miss Dinah are coming too."

The Hinkle sisters were planning to drive us since Momma's people had to get back to China Grove. Me and Momma headed for the car with Miss Pauline and Miss Dinah. But Lottie Scronce stopped us. She grabbed

Momma's arm. "Nobody," she said, "and I mean nobody, can sing 'Amazing Grace' the way your husband could. I sure will miss his singing."

I should've been glad people were reminding us of Pop's good points. But it seemed like they were trying hard to keep from saying what was on their minds—that when Pop died, he'd been out drinking.

Lottie turned away then, and I opened the car door for Momma. We settled into the back seat.

"Bessie," said Miss Dinah, "we're real thankful Axel fixed our car. Of course we insisted on paying him for his kindness, but we should have given the money to you instead."

Miss Pauline, who was driving, took her eyes off the road long enough to give Dinah one of her schoolteacher looks. I could tell she didn't like her sister bringing this up. But Dinah kept right on talking. "If we hadn't given him the money, maybe he'd have gone straight home that night."

It didn't take Momma two seconds to come back at Miss Dinah on that one. "Axel's death is not your fault," she said. "Seemed like the minute he had a few dollars in his pocket, he had to go over to Hog Hill and turn it into something bigger. Thing is, he never won at poker. Or if he did, he'd swap his winnings for Wayne Walker's corn liquor. And that's what killed him."

We got to the Honeycutts' then. Ann Fay was walking the front porch with baby Bobby up against her shoulder, patting him on the back. The twins were both sitting in the same rocker, watching for us. They jumped down and raced to the screen door to holler that we were there now. Leroy met us at the door.

There was food on the Hoosier cupboard and the cook stove too—roast chicken, potato salad, garden vegetables, pickles, and blackberry cobbler. We dished up our food and sat down to eat. The twins jabbered about this and that, and every now and again one of the grown-ups attempted to start up a conversation.

Miss Dinah tried to take our minds off Pop and the funeral. "Did you hear that Pauline retired? I can hardly believe she has finally extricated herself from teaching."

That sure did catch me by surprise. "You mean Miss Pauline won't be my teacher?"

"She heard you were coming," said Miss Dinah, "and decided to quit."

"Dinah!" said Miss Pauline. "I did no such thing. I wouldn't expect Junior to cause me a minute of trouble." She was embarrassed, I could tell. Truth was, I was glad she was retiring. I liked Miss Pauline fine, but it just wouldn't feel right to have my neighbor lady for my teacher.

When it was time to go, Myrtle sent the leftover food home with Momma. And when the Hinkle sisters dropped us off at our house, Miss Pauline pulled some money out of her purse and pushed it into Momma's hand. "This is what we paid Axel for the car repairs. It was intended to reach you, and I'm sure you can use it."

Momma shook her head, and the two of them went back and forth about who should have that ten-dollar bill. But Miss Pauline won the argument. Seemed like the neighbors were bent on taking care of us. I guessed everybody pitied us now. Or maybe they always had.

5

TUNE-UP
July 1941

A few days after we buried Pop, Leroy stopped by on his way home from work. "Do you or Bessie need anything? How're you doing, Junior?"

I shrugged. What was I supposed to say? *I'm mad because Pop is dead? I want to go sit on his grave and cuss at him the way he'd cuss at his father?*

It was better to change the subject. "Sounds like your truck still needs a tune-up."

He nodded. "Haven't had the time."

"I could fix that. I owe it to you. For looking after us the way you do."

Leroy squinted like he didn't think I could do such a thing without Pop's help.

"I've been watching him for years," I said, "memorizing every move he made."

Leroy nodded again. "I bet you have. All right, then. Come on down Saturday morning. Bring your pop's tools."

When I thought about working at Leroy's house, I

pictured his young'uns getting underfoot. "Or you could bring the truck here," I told him. "It'd be quieter."

Leroy looked up into the leaves of the big oak tree. Maybe he knew I'd do better work right there where I had learned from Pop. "That sounds fine. I'll come here."

On Saturday morning I'd just come back from milking Eleanor when I saw Leroy's truck pulling into the lane. And, dad gum, if Leroy didn't have Ann Fay with him! He drove past the house and parked under the oak.

"Morning, Leroy. I'll be with you just as soon as I strain this milk."

"Okey-doke. I'll go say hello to your momma." Leroy knocked on the back door and went on inside. Ann Fay hung around on the porch.

"Can I strain the milk?"

"No." I had half a notion to tell her to run home and help her momma if she wanted work to do.

"Why not?"

"Because. It's my job."

"Well, you could share it. I can do stuff, you know."

"Not this stuff." I put the cheesecloth over a gallon jug and tied a string around the mouth of the jar to hold it on. Then I poured the milk through. "Momma won't like it if she finds cow hairs or dirt in the milk."

Ann Fay folded her arms across her chest and turned and pouted her way to the steps. Jesse and Butch crowded up around her. Good. Maybe they'd keep her busy while me and Leroy worked.

But when we started up, of course Ann Fay had to be right there asking questions. "What do you call that thing, Daddy?" she asked. "What are spark plugs for, anyway?" Leroy didn't answer her because what man needs a young'un bothering him while he works? I learned a long time ago to watch and not talk when Pop was fixing a car.

But the thing about Leroy was, he didn't yell or let her agitate him. He just kept his mind on adjusting spark plugs. Ann Fay watched me clean one of the plugs—leaning in so close she nearly scrubbed it with her eyelashes. "I could do that," she said.

"Or you can learn the way I did. By watching." I lowered my voice so only she could hear. "Then when your daddy dies you'll know how to do it."

I shouldn't have said that on account of she was already worried about Leroy being called up for war—ever since Lottie Scronce's boy and some other local fellas were drafted. So I tried to take the words back. "Look," I said. "He ain't gonna die. Why don't you help Momma? She makes cakes on Saturday morning, and she'll let you sift the flour."

"I don't wanna sift flour. I wanna fix the truck." That's what she said, but I saw how the word *cake* lit a spark in Ann Fay's eye. She turned and flounced all angry-like into the house.

Finally, I could have some man-to-man time with Leroy.

Tuning up a car with him was nothing like working with Pop. He let me do about half of it, even gapping some of the spark plugs. About the time we were finishing, Ann Fay came out of the house. "Bessie said it's time for coffee and cake."

"Not yet," I told her. "We gotta crank this thing up and see how she sounds. In case we need to make adjustments."

I couldn't believe how fast Ann Fay opened that truck door and slid under the steering wheel. Evidently she thought she'd be the one to start it up.

I went to the window. "Hop out. This is my job."

Ann Fay didn't hop out. "Tell me when, Daddy," she hollered, "and I'll start it."

"You can't even reach the pedals," I told her.

"Wanna bet?" Ann Fay hung on to the steering wheel and pulled herself to the front of the seat. "Daddy showed me how to drive this truck." Maybe she was lying. But probably not. Ann Fay had wrapped herself around Leroy's little finger like icing on a cake.

Knowing that her daddy let her drive his truck got me all fired up. After all the cars I'd helped Pop fix! And he never, *ever* let me actually drive one of them. Now here she was, the little upstart, telling me her daddy had taught her to drive. She just had to come here and rub my nose in it, now didn't she?

6

GUILT
August 1941

The Friday evening before school started, we were on the porch and Momma was crocheting some doily thing. Seemed like when Pop died, she just made herself work harder. Crocheting every spare minute. And sewing for Mildred Rhinehart, who could afford to buy store-bought clothes for her daughter. If you asked me, Mildred just wanted an excuse to give Momma some money—without it looking like charity.

I decided the time for me to mention a job was now or never. "Pop said I should quit school."

Momma's crochet hook stopped. "You will not."

"But that's what he said. 'Get yourself a job and take care of your momma.' Almost like he knew he wasn't coming back."

Momma held up the lacy thing she was making. "See this antimacassar? I have orders for eight more. And I can sew and cook and clean houses, if I need to. How do you think we've been getting by all this time?" She put her foot down and the porch swing stopped moving. When it was at a dead stop she said, "I'll take care of us while you look after your education. You hear me, Junior?"

"Yes, Momma." But still, I wondered—why did Pop start talking that day about me dropping out of school? He brought it up twice, and I didn't remember him ever coming out and telling me that before. He must have known something was about to happen.

Maybe he just wanted to die. It seemed like the minute Granddaddy moved in, Pop started staying outside as much as possible. Taking his 12-gauge and going into the woods and ignoring me when I asked to go along. Later we'd hear gunshots and for some reason Momma would stop right in the middle of sifting flour and freeze until she heard another one. If she did, she'd start sifting again.

I don't think she even noticed she was doing that. But she must have been afraid of something. He hadn't shot himself. But could he have just decided to die?

"Momma?" I asked.

"Yes?"

"I've been wondering. Reckon he died to get away from Granddaddy?"

"Oh, my word and honor!" Momma threw both hands over her mouth, and that doily hit her in the face. I could see in her eyes as she stared at me that her mind was going over something I hadn't intended to put there. "You think—you—you think it's my fault, don't you?" she whispered.

"No! I didn't mean *that*, Momma. How could it be your fault?"

She just sat there shaking her head and holding her mouth like she was trying to keep from crying.

"I'm sorry, Momma. Forget I said it."

The words started spilling out of her. "After your granny died, Hammer would sit on the neighbors' porches, day in and day out, sniffing their cooking and inviting himself in for dinner. Pretty soon the people of Brookford had had enough. His own daughters refused to help! I felt it was our duty to take him in."

Momma's hands slid to her lap and her shoulders sagged. "I thought it would give Axel some self-respect," she said, "taking care of his daddy when his sisters wouldn't. But he was miserable from the minute Hammer got here. Oh, mercy. How will I *ever* forgive myself for this?" Momma put her head in her hands. "Axel, honey," she moaned. "I'm sorry. I should have listened to you."

Now I'd done it. I tried my best to take the words back, but I couldn't. Momma just kept saying how sorry she was. Finally she took her crocheting inside and disappeared into her room.

I wandered out to Pop's mechanic shop in the backyard. It wasn't a shop, really. Pop didn't have a garage to pull cars into. He just had that great big oak which gave him shade and helped slow down the raindrops when he needed it. There were ramps for driving cars onto and a block and tackle for pulling engines every now and again. There was a big spot of oil on the ground and two sweet potato crates for sitting on—if he ever took a break, which he almost never did.

I sat on a crate and breathed in the smell of the oak leaves and dirt and oil, and I just wanted him back. So what if he did all the fixing himself? Heck, I'd be holding the wrench out before he even asked. I wouldn't beg to start the engine or take the vehicle for a ride. I'd watch and learn and be glad for every minute of it.

Life with Pop hadn't been *all* bad. I thought about the good times, him joking one minute and singing "Amazing Grace" the next. As Lottie Scronce had said at Pop's funeral, he sure could sing that song. And he sang others, too—such as, "I Found a Million Dollar Baby (in a Five and Ten Cent Store)." He'd sing it to Momma when she was baking him a pecan pie or after she put on her Sunday hat. He sure knew how to put a spark in her eyes when he was in the mood.

I picked up an acorn and threw it, hard as I could, at the trunk of that oak tree. There was a big old knot there from where a limb had been cut off. I picked up another acorn and aimed it for the middle of that knot. And I kept throwing, harder and harder, like I could hurt that tree. But those puny little acorns just bounced off and landed on the ground, and the big old tree didn't know the difference.

They were like the questions he wasn't here to answer. *So what's the truth of it, Pop? Did you know you weren't coming back that night? What made you think you could just up and leave like that? I know you hated Granddaddy, and maybe you didn't even much care for me anymore, but couldn't you have stayed for Momma's sake? Hadn't you put her through enough already?*

Now I'd just added another burden onto Momma. Thanks to me, she believed that him dying was all her fault.

The next morning she was up early—baking like she expected the United States Army to stop in for dinner. She always said that making a mess in her kitchen helped bring order out of the muddle in her mind.

Granddaddy came around and poked his finger into her apple cake. "You should have got Inez to show you how to bake," he said.

Ever since Granddaddy moved in, Momma had been sweet as brown sugar to him, even when I wanted her to set him straight. Now her voice was bitter as baking soda. "If *only* your wife was here. Then you wouldn't have to eat my sorry cooking, would you, Hammer Bledsoe?"

It was like our conversation the night before had turned her against the old man.

Since I was the one who got Momma all riled up, I figured I could at least take him out from under her feet. "Come on, Granddaddy," I said. "Let's go check on the chickens. See how many eggs they've laid."

"I'm not going nowhere," said Granddaddy. "My bunions hurt." He plopped himself down at the kitchen table and started rubbing the knobby places that stuck out on the side of each foot. He also had hammer toes that arched up and under. If his feet felt as bad as they looked, I reckoned the pain in them was pretty ugly. But I didn't feel sorry for him.

I didn't think Momma pitied him either. She let him eat sweets all weekend, but whenever he tried to start up a conversation, she clamped her mouth shut. And when he asked for the time of day, she wouldn't give it.

7

SCHOOL
August 1941

After upsetting Momma like that, I sure didn't argue about school on Monday morning. On the way to the bus stop, I had myself a little talk with Pop—whether he could hear me or not.

"You're outvoted, Pop. Momma is bound and determined I should keep going. Besides, people respect education, and if there's one thing I intend to have, that's it. Respect."

On the school bus Ann Fay started jabbering first thing. "Too bad Miss Pauline quit—just when she was fixing to be your teacher."

"No," I said. "It's a good thing. Who wants their neighbor for their teacher?"

"But you could get by with stuff."

"Nope. You know how she is, Ann Fay. Even at home Miss Pauline has to have everything just the way she likes it. At school she's even more strict."

When Peggy Sue Rhinehart got on the bus, Ann Fay left me to sit with her. Those two sure did hit it off even if they were as opposite as hello and goodbye. Ann Fay was a tomboy, and Peggy Sue put me in mind of Shirley Temple with her curly blond hair and fancy bows. Today she was wearing one of those dresses Mildred had paid Momma to make. It had a matching hair bow.

When she stepped off the bus at school, Rob Walker ran up and yanked the bow right out of her hair.

Well, that just flew all over me—him picking on her for no reason. I jumped in and grabbed him by the arms. "You give that back."

Rob dropped the hair bow on the ground, and Ann Fay snatched it up and gave it to Peggy Sue.

That rascal was only a fourth grader trying to act like he was big and tough. But I was a high schooler. Same as his brother, Dudley, who happened to be right behind him now. Dudley took Rob by the arm and steered him away from me. "Pick on someone your own size," he told me.

"Hey, Catfish," I said. Catfish was his nickname. "I'm not picking on nobody. Your little brother was, though."

"Says you," Dudley snarled as he walked off with Rob. I headed to my class, feeling proud of myself for protecting Peggy Sue from a fourth-grade gangster.

I vowed I'd make a name for myself. One that didn't have anything to do with Axel Bledsoe. And if the other students had heard stories about Pop or bumped into him when he was sloppy drunk, well, I'd make them forget it.

But when I got to class, the good feelings left in a

hurry. It was like I was a tire and someone poked a great big hole in it so the air went rushing out. Because there, standing in front of the blackboard, was Miss Pauline.

"Good morning, Junior," she said.

"Uh, Miss Pauline—uh, uh," I stuttered, looking for something to say. Something that didn't let on how much I didn't want her to be my teacher. "Miss Pauline. I thought you retired."

"As it turned out, they couldn't find a replacement. My name, Junior Bledsoe, is Miss Hinkle."

"Yes, ma'am."

But how would I remember to call her that? Honestly, there should have been a law against having your neighbor as your teacher.

The bell rang, and Miss Pauline told us to find the desks she'd marked out for us. And to practice the drills on page 85 of the books on our desks.

My seat was second to the front. Miss Pauline—er, Miss Hinkle—had placed a brand-new composition book there with my full name on it, *Axel Bledsoe, Junior*, written in her perfect longhand. The pencil groove on the desk held a new pencil, sharpened to a fine point. And there was the small brown book I'd seen every year since third grade, *The Palmer Method of Business Writing*.

Did high schoolers still have to practice handwriting?

That cotton-pickin' book didn't just tell you how to make the letters. It told you how to sit and where to place your arms and which hand to hold your pencil in. It sure didn't have a page for what to do if your left hand worked better than your right one. Some teachers were nice enough to let me use my left hand, especially if they were left-handed themselves. But Miss Pauline wasn't, and I knew, without asking, that she was the kind of teacher who went by the book.

I turned to page 85, put the pencil in my right hand, and read the sentences on that page.

Always study drill before practicing.
Be sure to use a good rapid movement.
Do not fail to see and correct all errors.

Miss Hinkle called the roll. First came Janie Aderholt, who sat right in front of me. I was second. "Axel Bledsoe, Junior," Miss Hinkle called out.

I heard a snort in the back of the room and turned to see who it came from. Dudley Walker. I never did like Dudley. Or Rob, who didn't wash behind his ears and was always picking on someone. And I sure didn't care for their no-good father, who'd sold moonshine to Pop.

Then I started thinking Dudley had probably heard something from his daddy about what went on at Hog Hill that night. As soon as I could, I'd ask him what he knew about Pop dying.

Miss Pauline called Calvin Settlemyre's name, but of course he wasn't there. Evidently his parents hadn't bothered to notify Mountain View School that he'd dropped out. I raised my hand. "Miss Pau—I mean, Miss Hinkle, Calvin quit school."

She frowned. "If this is true, then it is indeed most unfortunate."

At lunchtime I sat down across from Dudley. "Howdy, Catfish," I said. Dudley was busy flirting with Janie Aderholt and her friend Marilyn Overcash. But from the looks on their faces I could tell they needed an excuse to give him the cold shoulder.

Janie stood. "We'll let y'all boys talk in private," she said. And just like that, she and Marilyn scooped up their trays and moved to another table.

"Sorry," I said. "I must've scared them off."

Dudley glared. "You *look* sorry."

I shrugged and got down to business. "I reckon my pop caught a ride with yours the night he died."

Dudley had a big old sour pickle and was just ready to take a bite. But he stopped with it in midair. "I reckon you *don't* know, now do ya?"

"I know who has a fast car so he can outrun the law. And who was always more than happy to give my pop a ride and take his money any day of the week. Which he didn't have much of, by the way. How come your daddy didn't bring him home that night? Did they have a fight or something?"

Dudley shrugged and bit into the pickle. Yellow juice ran out of the corner of his mouth, and he wiped it with the back of his hand. "You're barking up the wrong tree. I don't know nothing."

"Well then, Catfish, maybe you can find out. And when you do, how about letting me know?"

Of course he had to put in the last word. "Just so you know, only my friends call me Catfish. And, from the sound of things, you ain't one of them."

"Right," I muttered. "And I don't wanna be."

The truth was, even if I didn't much like Dudley, we'd never been out-and-out enemies. But that was before Pop died. Right now I needed someone to blame for his passing, and as far as I could tell, Dudley's father was the most likely culprit. I just needed Dudley to help me get to the bottom of things.

8

ATTACK
September 1941

"Ready. Aim. Fire!" That was Granddaddy talking. He followed up with a string of words I wouldn't repeat.

His cussing woke me the rest of the way. I opened one eye. Straight ahead of me I saw Granddaddy's knobby white feet dangling from the bed. His thick toenails looked like they hadn't been trimmed since Granny died.

"It's about time you rouse yourself. You fixin' on sleeping through the war?"

I sat up. "Did the president declare war while I was sleeping?"

Granddaddy cussed again. "One of these days he'll be forced to get himself a backbone."

"Oh." So we *weren't* in the war yet after all.

Granddaddy caught me up on the news. "Iceland. The Germans attacked an American ship. But we fired back. Yes siree! Wish I was on that ship. I'd blast those Krauts to Hades and back." Granddaddy turned the radio up so I couldn't miss the news even if I wanted to.

And part of me did want to. I wished I could wake up

in the morning with nothing bigger than homework to worry about. I pulled the pillow over my head as if that would make the world and all its problems go away. If hiding under the covers would keep war from coming to America, I'd stay there all day.

Getting out of bed was hard anyway. These days nobody asked me how I was doing. Even if they had, I couldn't have explained it. Pop had been gone almost two months and I should be used to it by now. But some days I still couldn't believe he was dead. Except that he never came home. And I had to milk Eleanor twice a day and try to be the man of the house. And put up with Granddaddy.

He was still yelling about war. What would it be like to have my own bed back? And to dress in the morning in a little peace and quiet? Finally, after five minutes of him raving, I crawled out of bed. "Yeah. *I* wish you was on that ship too."

I didn't say it real loud, but he heard it. "You getting smart with me?" Granddaddy reached for his shoe. "You want war, I'll show you war."

Before I figured out what he was up to, that shoe came flying at my nose. "Whoa!" That hurt! "Granddaddy. I don't want war." I pulled my britches on, grabbed my shirt and shoes, and left the room.

"Heaven help!" said Momma. "Your nose is bleeding." She wet a washcloth with cold water and clamped it against my face.

"That old man threw a shoe at me. I'm not going back in there. I'll sleep on the porch first."

"Of course you won't sleep on the porch." Momma lowered her voice. "Maybe we'll put Granddaddy outside." She snickered.

But she didn't mean it. She'd moved him in and now that Pop was gone she didn't want him anymore. But how could we get rid of him?

On the school bus I stared out the window so Ann Fay would know to leave me alone. What was wrong with that old man, anyway? Sometimes it felt like war wasn't across the ocean. It was right there in my own house. And inside me too. I didn't know which way to think or feel, and I didn't know who to be angry with. Pop for leaving or Granddaddy for staying. Or Momma for being bighearted and taking him in.

I started imagining Granddaddy sitting in that seat by the bus window and me in the driver's seat. I'd speed right past Mountain View School and down the hill into Brookford. He'd find himself on Aunt Lucille's porch quicker than he could say *Yankee Doodle Dandy*.

School started out like usual—with Miss Hinkle lecturing us on handwriting. "You cannot hope to be successful if you do not use proper technique." She adjusted her dark-rimmed glasses and stared smack dab at me. "There is no excuse for letters that lean to the left."

I knew she'd figured out I sometimes did my homework with my left hand.

I opened my composition book and picked up my pencil with my right hand. My mind went back to me and Pop target-practicing with the BB gun. He was a lefty too, but he did all his hunting from the right shoulder. "Them who make guns don't give two hoots about left handers," he used to say. "So you gotta practice. After a while it'll come natural as a dog scratching at fleas."

I kept his advice in mind while I practiced the movement drills she'd written on the blackboard. Miss Hinkle walked the aisles, her shoes clicking on the wooden floor and her voice grating like chalk on the board. "Rolling muscular movement is the best. Keep thinking. Keep moving. Keep gliding."

How was I supposed to think anything with her slipping around like a German U-boat ready to attack? Only thing was, Miss Hinkle wasn't sneaky like a submarine. I knew right when she was coming toward me. Still, I jumped when she reached across my desk and flipped a few pages in the handwriting book. She tapped her fingers on a photograph of children writing. "See how those students are situated? Mimic their posture."

"Yes, ma'am," I said. I couldn't even *sit* right for Miss Pauline.

Sometimes it just felt that *I* was all wrong—born into the wrong family with a pop who drank too much and couldn't keep the bills paid up. On top of all that, I didn't even use the same hand everybody else used. Whether I liked it or not, those things were me. Pop wasn't perfect, for sure, but he was my father and there were good things about him that others just didn't see.

"I will expect you to practice over the weekend, Junior. Take the book home and do the first five drills until they become second nature to you."

"Yes, ma'am," I said. I knew what second nature meant, but I liked the way Pop said it better. I'd seen plenty of dogs scratching at fleas.

After school, before I even did my chores, I went to my room, gathered up my featherbeds and my pillow, and headed out the door.

"Where you think you're going?" asked Granddaddy.

"Back porch. Where it's peaceful."

"You'll miss the Yankees and the Red Sox."

"Yup." I wasn't about to let on like I cared.

Momma was just putting her washtubs away when I got to the porch. "What are you doing?"

"Protecting myself. I've had enough of that old man."

"You'll freeze out here."

"Momma, it's nowhere near freezing and I've got Jesse and Butch to keep me warm. I know you're not going to put Granddaddy out here. Did he apologize for throwing that shoe at me?"

Momma turned away. I could tell she hadn't talked to him. She was probably scared of what it would start up. As long as he was quiet, she wouldn't upset him if she could help it.

Going to bed that night, I actually heard most of the

baseball game through the bedroom wall. Granddaddy banged on the iron bedstead whenever the Yankees batted in a run. "Reckon you heard that, didn't ya?" he'd yell. It was almost like he missed having me in there to share the game with.

Joe DiMaggio didn't play, but his brother Dom got a hit and a run for the Red Sox. Still, the Yankees won 6–3. And just like that, Granddaddy started snoring.

More games were broadcast on Saturday and Sunday nights, and he made sure I heard them too. Even if he hadn't turned the volume up, I would've known what was going on because of him yelling at the players.

Baseball was big in Granddaddy's book, but war was even bigger. On Tuesday evening, he reminded us that the President was speaking to the American people about the problem of German submarines.

Momma pulled two chairs up outside the bedroom door.

"Shh," said Granddaddy. "How am I supposed to hear him declare war?"

President Roosevelt said that in spite of what Hitler claimed, the Germans had attacked the USS *Greer* first. That the Nazis wanted to control the seas and were watching to see if America would give them a green light on their path of destruction.

"*One peaceful nation after another,*" President Roosevelt said, "*has met disaster because each refused to look the Nazi danger squarely in the eye until it actually had them by the throat. The United States will not make that fatal mistake."*

Granddaddy pounded the arm of his rocking chair and talked back at the radio. "Then what *are* you going to do about it, Mr. President?"

"Shh," said Momma.

"But when you see a rattlesnake poised to strike," said the President, *"you do not wait until he has struck before you crush him. These Nazi submarines and raiders are the rattlesnakes of the Atlantic."* He went on to say that if our ships encountered German or Italian boats in American waters of self-defense from now on, our men had orders to shoot.

Waters of self-defense. According to the papers we had plenty of ships out there protecting places Hitler was trying to take over. And German submarines were sneaking all around, ready to strike.

Most people believed that once Hitler conquered Europe, he'd be coming after America. If we didn't shoot on sight he'd think he could take us over, too. But no siree! America was the land of the free. And we intended to keep it that way. Even if it meant all-out war.

I was pretty sure that's exactly what was about to break loose.

9

SHOOT ON SIGHT
October 1941

Just when I had the .22 aimed at his head, I heard a voice. Of course the squirrel scrambled to the back side of the tree, and I missed my chance. Who in tarnation was in the woods with me?

I peeked through the small holly tree, and not far away was Ann Fay with Leroy. He had a finger over his lips, reminding her to be quiet. I could see they had their eyes on my squirrel!

The crunchy sound of their feet on the dry leaves took me way back, to when I was eight years old. And their white breath clouds in the cool air—it was like being there again, in the woods with Pop, learning to shoot squirrel for the first time.

Leroy whispered to Ann Fay about this and that, pointing to the sights on the gun. I heard Pop's voice in my head. *The sights are there to help you line it up. But don't look at the sights. Keep your eye on the target.*

The squirrel was still on the back side of the tree,

and I knew it wouldn't come around for a while now. I figured Ann Fay couldn't be still for as long as it would take to wait it out.

Didn't she have two sisters and a baby brother to look after? What was she doing out here with her daddy? Sometimes it seemed like that man never went anywhere without taking his precious Ann Fay along. For some reason the sight of them together first thing in the morning just provoked me.

I raised my rifle again. I hadn't left the house before daylight for nothing. The way I saw things, that squirrel belonged to me.

Fifteen minutes or so later, the squirrel still hadn't come back into view. Ann Fay was probably fixing to bust wide open, but I didn't look. I just kept my eye on that tree. Then I saw a motion—a bushy tail flickering. The squirrel ran out along a branch and stopped. Perfect. I steadied my gun and got him in my sights. I pulled the trigger. And just like that, it fell.

Ann Fay screamed, and from the sound of it, you would think I'd shot *her*. To be honest, I took some satisfaction out of scaring her good and proper. When I stepped out from behind the holly, there she was, not twenty feet away, with her hand over her mouth. Leroy looked just about as startled as she did.

"Morning," I called. "Sure didn't mean to scare you."

"Junior Bledsoe! You stole my squirrel." Ann Fay was

hopping mad. So mad she looked like she might cry.

But why should I feel sorry for her? Didn't she have a daddy to help her get the next one?

I headed toward them but waved my hand in the direction of the squirrel. "Skin it and you can have it, Ann Fay." I figured that would stop her in her tracks. Although if she took me up on it, Leroy would probably teach her how to do it.

Leroy shook his head. "It's yours, Junior. Didn't know you were over here."

I nodded. "Momma wants to make squirrel pie. So I got up before the chickens."

Leroy ruffled Ann Fay's hair. "Sleepyhead here had trouble waking up."

Ann Fay was blinking back tears. Maybe I shouldn't have shot the squirrel, knowing she was after it. But then again, if she wanted to run around in the woods like a man, she might have to take disappointment like a man too.

But I didn't tell her that. "There's lots of squirrels in these woods, Ann Fay. I bet you'll bring down the next one you see. I'll leave and give you some peace and quiet. That way I won't get hit with that .22 you got there."

I was trying to make a joke, but she didn't laugh. Leroy didn't either. "Don't you worry," he said. "This girl is learning to aim real good."

"I bet so." I waved goodbye and went after my

squirrel. If Leroy had anything to say about it, that girl would learn to hunt or drive or do whatever she set her mind to. It didn't used to bother me how close the two of them were, but now that Pop was gone, sometimes it just felt like a slap in my face.

10

HOSTILITY
October 1941

We'd been riding to church with the Honeycutts ever since Leroy came home with that truck. Momma squeezed in up front with Myrtle, Leroy, and baby Bobby. Ann Fay and I sat in the back holding the twins between our knees to keep them from bouncing around in the truck.

Usually we'd sing silly songs. But today, Ann Fay was not in a Sunday-morning mood. We were barely on the highway when she let me know it. "You stole my squirrel, Junior Bledsoe."

"Shoot, Ann Fay! I was in the woods first."

"How do *you* know?"

"Because. I got up before daylight. And I was all ready to shoot that squirrel when, all of a sudden, I heard you talking."

"See? You knew I was there. You could've been bighearted and left it for me."

"And let you scare it off? I reckon you think it's all hunky-dory for you and your daddy to go squirrel hunting together. But don't forget, you're a girl. I'm the man at my house now and we needed some meat."

After that, the two of us stopped talking and Ida started begging me for a song. "Okay, okay." I said. It wasn't raining, but I just sang what popped in my head. *"It's raining, it's pouring. The old man is snoring. He went to bed and he bumped his head and didn't wake up in the morning."*

The girls giggled and made snoring noises the rest of the way to church. It was a silly song, but if you stopped and thought about it, there wasn't anything funny about the words.

At church Leroy parked beside Ralph Settlemyre's truck. I used to ride in the back of that truck when me and Pop went night-fishing with Ralph and Calvin. That seemed like a really long time ago. I tried to catch up with Calvin on the way to Sunday school, but by the time I got there he was talking to the other fellows about turkey hunting with his daddy.

It seemed like I couldn't turn around without somebody rubbing my nose in the fact that I didn't have a father anymore. I knew it wasn't what they intended. It's just the way it was.

At least when Pop was alive we could go out together and make it look like we were a regular family. Some days we just gussied up and went to church, pretending.

After Sunday school we all filed into church and sat with our families. Reverend Price announced that Lottie Scronce's second son had just been drafted into the army.

He prayed for the Scronce boys to be safe and for all the people who were called to serve.

"Each of us must be prepared to defend freedom however we're needed," said the reverend. He started in on how bad the world was these days with Hitler slaughtering millions of people. Italy was right there helping him, and Japan was every bit as greedy as Germany, the way they were trying to take over China and all the other Orientals.

I could almost hear Pop grumbling over Sunday dinner. "Another doomsday sermon," he'd say—if only he were still here. That's what he called it whenever Reverend Price preached about the world coming to an end.

While the reverend preached, I spotted a rubber band on the floor under the pew in front of me. I reached down and picked it up. It gave me something to fiddle with. During the closing prayer, when most people had their eyes closed, I looked at Ann Fay sitting two rows ahead of me. She had her head against her daddy's shoulder.

I remembered the scratchy feel of Pop's wool coat sleeve against my cheek. Every once in a while he'd give me something to play with during preaching—his watch on a chain, his pocketknife, or a pen and paper. But then I turned eleven and he started shrugging me off. It was like my birthday came and he walked away from me.

What would it be like to be ten again? With me leaning on Pop's arm?

I could see the back of Ann Fay's neck where her hair had separated. I don't know why I wanted to send that rubber band whizzing for that white spot. I didn't spend a lot of time thinking about whether it was a good idea. I just made my hand into a gun shape and wrapped the rubber band between my thumb and trigger finger. Then I aimed and let it fly.

Zing! I hit her smack dab on that spot of flesh. And boy did she yelp! Baby Bobby, who'd been snoozing on Myrtle's shoulder, woke up screaming. Just like that, the reverend stopped praying.

I closed my eyes real fast.

But I could hear Myrtle shushing the baby. I imagined Leroy pulling Ann Fay close and looking at the spot on her neck. I sure hoped my face wasn't as red as I thought it was. Someone giggled. Reverend Price went back to his prayer and finished up, and the choir sang a final song—*"Onward Christian soldiers, marching as to war . . ."*

I tried to leave real quick. But when I got to the end of the pew, Peggy Sue was there waiting on me. "Junior Bledsoe, how could you do such a thing?"

"What?" I tried to sound innocent.

"You know what I'm talking about. I saw you shoot Ann Fay with that rubber band."

"Good grief! What are you, a German spy? It was an accident, Peggy Sue. And anyway, you're supposed to have your eyes shut when the preacher is praying."

"Huh! Practice what you preach, Junior Bledsoe."

People were going past us, but Leroy and Ann Fay were standing right in front of me. Leroy had his hand on her neck, and I could see his thumb making soft circles on that spot where the rubber band hit her. He reached his other hand to me, and there, wrapped around his fingers, was that rubber band. "Did you lose something, Junior?"

"Sir, I'm sorry. I didn't mean to do it." That sounded just stupid and I knew it, but still, I tried to explain. "I don't know what came over me. I didn't plan it. It just happened."

Leroy nodded. "See that it doesn't happen again." His voice was cold as an icebox.

Momma spoke up then. "I'm sorry, Leroy. Junior won't get by with this." She jabbed my arm. "Tell Ann Fay you're sorry."

From the look in Ann Fay's eye, I was sure she didn't want to hear *sorry* coming out of my mouth. She'd rather be mad at me. That girl sure had some fight in her. But I took a deep breath and said, "I'm sorry, Ann Fay. I didn't mean it. Honest, I didn't."

Ann Fay folded her arms across her chest and gave me a look that would take the pelt right off a squirrel. "I guess you think I believe that, Junior Bledsoe? Well, I don't."

"I will see that Junior gets his just desserts," said Momma.

Sometimes Momma had a strange way of putting things. Dessert today was the sweet potato pie she'd made for Sunday dinner. But she wasn't talking about that, because I couldn't have any. In fact, she made me miss dinner altogether.

"You're spending the afternoon in your bedroom, but first I expect you to go outside and gather up your blankets and pillow. No more sleeping on the porch for you."

"Momma! That's not fair. Me shooting that rubber band doesn't have anything to do with Granddaddy. He's mean as a rattlesnake and I can't share a room with him."

"You can and you will," said Momma. "I won't have you catching your death by sleeping outside." She threw open the back door and stood there with one hand on her hip and the other pointing to the corner of the porch where I'd been sleeping.

"I'm not going."

Momma didn't argue. Instead she went outside and came back loaded down with bedding. She stopped not two feet away and looked me dead in the eye. "Your pillow is still out there. Get it. I've lost one man to stupidity, and I do not intend to lose another for acting the fool." Her chin started wobbling, and for some reason my determination did too.

By the time I came inside with my pillow she was shoving bedroom furniture back to where it belonged because Granddaddy had taken over the whole room. Now he looked like he was fixing to raise Cain.

"Don't you say a word, Hammer Bledsoe," said

Momma. "I'm of half a mind to move Junior in and you out. So if you want a roof over your head and food in your belly, I suggest you move that radio back to your side of the room and be quiet."

Granddaddy shut his mouth. He didn't say a word, not even to me, when Momma went to the cedar chest for clean sheets.

When my bed on the floor was made up and she was gone, I flopped down and pulled the pillow over my head. I was not in the mood for listening to the Melody Boys singing gospel hymns on the radio. I thought about Ann Fay. She must wonder what she'd done to deserve the way I'd treated her lately.

Nothing, I thought. I mean, nothing except being a girl and a chatterbox too. But ever since Pop died, just the sight of her and Leroy together made me want to smack something with my fist. I knew it wasn't her fault Pop was gone. He had sort of been gone ever since my eleventh birthday.

Even with the pillow over my head I could still hear the radio. Now someone was talking about Japan being mad at the United States for cutting off oil supplies. Some politician was of the opinion that Japan was likely to start a war with us.

Granddaddy kept changing the stations. It was like he was carrying on his own private war, listening to one station praising peace negotiations with Japan and another one saying the Japanese would not stop until they owned all the islands of the Pacific Ocean, including the ones that America laid claim to.

"Look for an attack from the Japanese," said Granddaddy. "Them Japs are sneaky. Our president had better hit them before they hit us."

Sometime during the afternoon I fell asleep. I dreamed that Japanese soldiers were sneaking around in our yard. They had me and Momma trapped in the house and Pop locked up in the shed. I could hear him out there calling for us. Momma was trying to get out the front door and I was at the back, but the doorknob was stuck. And I kept yelling for Pop to come fix that doorknob so I could go out to him.

It didn't make sense, but that's how dreams are. When I woke up, Granddaddy was singing along with the radio. "*There'll be peace in the valley for me . . .*"

Nothing made sense in real life either.

That afternoon, the Yankees won the fourth game in the World Series. DiMaggio got a hit. He'd broken his streak back in July, about a week after Pop died. But he was still golden in my book because, for a little while during each game, he got Granddaddy shouting about something besides America going to war.

11

RESPECT
October 1941

Miss Pauline was explaining dangling participles. If you asked me, she wasn't doing a good job of it, because I wasn't catching on. But all of a sudden, I heard my name. "Junior, can you give us an example?"

"Uh—no, Miss Pauline. I don't think so."

I heard Dudley snort and everyone else start to laugh, and that's when I realized I had just called her Miss Pauline.

"I'm sorry. I meant to say 'Miss Hinkle.' I really did."

Miss Hinkle squinted her eyes real narrow and pressed her lips together and stared. She waited until everyone in the class stopped snickering, and then she finally spoke. "Mr. Bledsoe, I want you to write three paragraphs on the importance of respect. You may do this while the others are eating lunch."

"Yes, Miss Hinkle." I heard Dudley making snickering noises again.

"Dudley, since you find this so amusing, you may join him."

The rest of the class went to eat and we sat in the room, writing. Or trying to, anyway. I stared at my paper. Time was passing and my belly was growling and I'd only written three sentences. I tapped the page with my pencil, as if *that* would make some words come out of it.

Respect. If I was to write what I really thought about that word, I'd say it was something other people had and I wanted. I'd write that respectable people seemed to look down on the rest of us but maybe that was because they didn't know what we were going through. And that if certain people knew how Momma had stood by Pop, maybe they'd respect her more. If there was anybody in the world who deserved some respect, it was Bessie Bledsoe.

But I didn't write any of that. First of all, Miss Hinkle probably knew most of it already, and second, she wasn't talking about that kind of respect. She wanted me to say something about how we weren't just neighbors anymore. How she was my teacher and I should remember to treat her as such. I should say *Yes, ma'am* and *No, ma'am* and *Please* and *Thank you* and *Excuse me*, at all the right times. I should sit up straight and not write my name on my desk or make tapping sounds with my toe when other people were trying to think.

I snuck a peek at Dudley. He was staring into space and chewing on his pencil. "What you looking at?" he snarled. "Mind your own beeswax."

After the first day of school I hadn't said a word

to Dudley about his daddy and the night my pop died. Mostly I avoided him because I had enough to think about without arguing with someone I'd rather not talk to. But now, since he seemed determined to pick a fight with me, I went along with it. "It's about time you tell me what your old man was doing on the night my pop died. What'd you find out?"

"Like I said, mind your own business."

"What happened to my pop *is* my business. And I better not find out your sorry old man had anything to do with it."

Dudley let on like he hadn't even heard me.

I had half a notion to go stand over top of him until he paid me some respect. I was fixing to do just that when the class came back from lunch.

Miss Hinkle took one look at my paper. "First of all," she said, "it appears that you've been twiddling your thumbs instead of writing. And second, your handwriting leaves much to be desired. Were you using your left hand?"

"Yes, ma'am," said Dudley. "He sure was."

The truth was, I didn't remember which hand I used. I'd been worrying too much about what to write.

Miss Hinkle ignored Dudley. "I want you to finish this, Junior. And then rewrite it. Your small *t*'s should not have loops in them." She quoted from that confounded handwriting book. "*Do not fail to see and correct all errors.*"

"Yes, Miss Hinkle." I sure didn't know when she thought I'd have time to rewrite a whole page, plus do my other work.

When I got home, I hadn't even changed into everyday clothes when Momma came up with jobs for me. "The sweet potatoes have to be dug before we get frost," she said. "And we'll need a whole lot more firewood before winter sets in."

I knew that. But knowing it didn't mean I had time for doing it. Between Momma and Miss Hinkle I was covered over with more work than one person could possibly do.

But I dug the sweet potatoes and carried them to the back porch. After I cleaned up, I finished the essay. I still had to copy it over in my best Palmer longhand. But my brain and my muscles were plumb worn out for one day. So I put it off until the next morning.

12

FRUSTRATION
October 1941

I crawled out of bed early and worked at the kitchen table. The more I thought about that pencil in my right hand, the more I wanted to switch it to my left. But with every word leaning in the wrong direction, Miss Hinkle would know.

Momma came into the kitchen in her nightgown and bed jacket and Pop's thick wool socks—squinting against the light. "You're up early."

"Homework."

She hugged her bed jacket close around her. "And you couldn't load the woodstove first?"

"Wasn't thinking. Just trying to do my homework." I left my paper on the table and went to the porch for wood. Pop would've had the fire laid last night so all he had to do this morning was stir the ashes and blow on them to light the kindling.

Unless he was out drinking, of course.

Momma didn't seem to notice that all his jobs had been left to me. I carried in wood and lit the fire and went back to copying that essay. I was just starting the last paragraph when she started fretting again. "Are you watching the clock?"

"I'll be done in a minute, Momma."

"You still have animals to tend to. Breakfast is ready." Momma set a bowl of hot grits beside me and when she did they splashed onto my paper. I jumped up. "Look what you did!" I yelled. "Miss Hinkle will make me do it all over again. And when am I supposed to do that? Between all the firewood and tending animals and doing whatever else Pop left for me to do, it's a wonder I have time to go to the outhouse."

I didn't look at Momma, but I could tell she'd gone still as a statue.

"I'll go milk." I grabbed the bucket and my coat and escaped out the back door.

It was warmer in the barn with the animals. I fed Grover first and leaned against his neck for comfort. "I'm sorry I haven't been paying you any mind," I said. "But my life is plumb crazy. I can hardly find time to feed my own face. Maybe I should skip school today. Then you and me—we could take a ride up the mountain."

Of course I couldn't skip school. That would just provoke Momma even more. After milking Eleanor, I carried the bucket inside. "I don't have time to strain it."

"I'll do that for you," said Momma. "I wrote a note to Miss Pauline, explaining about your paper and all you have on your shoulders right now. Eat your breakfast."

Ten minutes later, I started out the door with her pushing my arms into my jacket sleeves. "I'm sorry, son," she said. "I don't mean to weigh you down. But there's work to be done and *your pop* isn't here to do it."

There was a bitterness to the way she said *your pop*. I had this feeling she wasn't claiming him just then. That somehow I deserved all the work he went off and left for me to pick up. Maybe it was true. Because, as far as I could remember, he never drank before my eleventh birthday. It must have been my fault he started drinking.

Momma handed me my lunch bag and then my books, and when she did, a tear splashed onto my hand. "Go on," she said, "before you miss your bus."

13

WAR MANEUVERS
November 1941

I was sound asleep when all of a sudden I heard a commotion under the house. Jesse and Butch were making the awfullest racket, which meant someone had to be coming in on our property.

"Tell them dogs to shut up!" yelled Granddaddy.

I sat up and saluted in his direction. "Yes, sir!" I reached for my overalls and pulled them on over my long handles. After stuffing my feet into my shoes, I headed for the living room and looked out the window. I couldn't see much for all the cedar trees between our house and the road, but I saw movement out there, and I declare, from all the vehicle noises it sounded like the United States Army was moving in.

Jesse and Butch were by the cedars, fixing to bark their own ears off. I headed out there, hollering for them to hush, but they didn't pay me any mind. They probably didn't hear me for all the noise.

When I rounded the bend by the cedars I almost fell over. Going right past our yard was one army jeep after another. And not just jeeps but tanks and even motorcycles. It was like the war had come right there to our front yard.

The soldiers riding by were grinning. Some of them, anyway. Others looked serious as a storm. One saluted as he rattled past on an army tank. Another laughed and elbowed his buddy. They lifted their caps and ran their fingers through their hair, and I realized they were poking fun at me. I must have looked a sight with my hair going every which way and my eyes barely open.

I wondered if I was even awake. Maybe I was dreaming. Because what in the world were soldiers doing here, heading toward Bakers Mountain?

Right behind me I heard a voice. Granddaddy's voice. And boy did he sound happy. "Yee haw! The United States Army has come to town."

The old man had barely left the house since he moved in. And now, there he was standing by the road, straight as a light pole with his hand at his forehead, saluting. He had his right stub over his heart.

A soldier jumped off one of the tanks and ran up to Granddaddy. "Sir," he said, "I should be saluting you. I believe you served in the Great War." His eyes fastened on Granddaddy's stub.

Something happened to Granddaddy's face then. It went from being serious and proud to just kind of slack and sad. But only for a second, until he caught himself. Then he cussed and shook the soldier off. His arms dropped to his sides, and he turned and stalked back toward the house.

The soldier looked confused. "I offended him. I didn't intend to. I wanted to thank him."

"Never mind him," I said. "He's cantankerous that way. What's happening? Am I dreaming?"

The soldier laughed. "Having a nightmare, more likely. We're practicing for war. Didn't you hear? Someone should have informed you the army was moving in." He nodded toward Bakers Mountain. "Looks like you and me'll be neighbors for a few days." He offered his hand. "Private Frank Jenkins. Call me Frank."

"Yes, sir. I'm Junior. Bledsoe. We're mighty proud to have you, sir. Are you really practicing for war?"

He nodded. "I'm on the Blue Team. We represent one country. Our enemy, the Red Team, is heading up the other side of the mountain. We'll be practicing our skills and testing our equipment, which is pitiful. Some of those boys are carrying wooden guns. I had a real one, but one of the Reds stole it in a maneuver in Davidson County."

I thought I was starting to get the picture. These boys were playing war, like I used to on the playground at school. Or all by myself with my BB gun and imaginary enemies stalking the woods behind our barn. It hit me then how I could help. "You need a gun?" I asked. "Wait a minute and I'll bring you one."

I ran to the house. "We're being invaded by the United States Army," I said.

Momma was shoving firewood into the stove. She pushed the door shut and straightened up in a cloud of smoke. "Junior, what *are* you talking about? And why is Hammer fit to be tied?"

"Army maneuvers, right here on Bakers Mountain. I talked to one of the fellas, and he needs a gun."

"The army doesn't supply their own weapons? Why do they need guns? They can't be shooting each other."

"They're not loaded, Momma. Some of them have wooden guns. Toys. I'll give him my BB gun."

Momma stared. "Your pop gave that to you."

I realized that. And big as I was, I wasn't excited about losing that gun. But this was the war we were talking about. Real soldiers were practicing outside my door, and they needed equipment. Seemed like the least I could do was hand over a toy I should've outgrown by now. I reached for my box of BBs on the shelf.

I turned away before Momma could get me all sentimental. The shotgun and the rifle were there too. Maybe I should take them.

"Better hurry," said Momma, "or they'll be gone."

I could still hear the motorcycles out there. And Jesse and Butch barking to beat the band. Howling, actually. I ran out the front door, and by the time I reached the cedars the dogs had settled down. No wonder—Ann Fay was there with Jesse under one arm and Butch under the other. Leroy stood just behind her with his hands on her shoulders.

Up the road, other neighbors were lining up to watch the excitement. Frank Jenkins was by the mailbox watching for me. "Sir," I said, "it's not much, but maybe it's better than no gun at all." I fished the box of BBs from my pocket.

His eyes lit up like he was a young'un being handed an RC Cola. "I shall be the envy of my entire outfit," he said. "I have a buddy who's played one too many pranks on me, and he's about to be bit in the butt." Frank winked and tucked the BBs in his pocket. "After hours, of course."

14

TROUBLE
November 1941

War maneuvers on Bakers Mountain lasted over the weekend. We'd hear shouting and vehicle noises coming from the mountain, and at night we'd see the glow of campfires.

People came from miles around delivering hand-knitted socks and gloves and even cakes to the fellows—the ones on patrol, that is. The ones who weren't involved in combat up on the mountain.

The colored church next door to us made a big bonfire. Curiosity seekers warmed themselves by it and chatted with some of the army men. And the choir stood on the steps of the church and sang, *"It's me, O Lord, standing in the need of prayer."*

The army men left on Sunday evening. I headed out to the road to watch them go, but first Momma pushed some cookies and two pairs of knit socks into my hands. "Take these," she said.

I met Frank coming up our lane. "Here's your gun,"

he said. "I haven't had so much fun since I signed up. I'm afraid I used all the BBs, though."

"You aren't keeping the gun?"

"We just got word our supplies are in, so I won't be needing it. But you sure boosted troop morale." Frank pounded my back. "Now you can say you did your bit for the war."

The next morning at school, the only thing people wanted to talk about was army maneuvers. Miss Hinkle even skipped handwriting exercises to discuss our experiences. Marilyn Overcash and other students who lived on the back side of the mountain had talked with soldiers from the Red Team. According to them, the Reds had won the "Battle of Bakers Mountain."

It hadn't even crossed my mind to ask who won. "I loaned my BB gun to a soldier," I said.

"BB gun?" Dudley snorted, and everybody else in the room seemed to think it was a big joke too.

I tried to defend myself. "The army is short on supplies. Some of those fellows were using toy guns. And the soldier I gave the gun to was thrilled. Said it boosted troop morale."

"Isn't that sweet?" said Dudley.

A few other people snickered. And for some reason all the good feelings I had about troop morale just crumbled like dry cornbread.

"Junior makes a good point," said Miss Hinkle.

"Supplying the army is a massive undertaking. I hope your families have contributed unused metals and empty tin cans to the scrap drives."

This led to a discussion about the economic depression our country had been in. And not just America, but the world. According to Miss Hinkle, the depression led Germany to follow a maniac like Adolf Hitler. The German people were desperate for a leader who could turn their economy around.

Miss Hinkle asked us to compare and contrast Adolf Hitler's methods with President Roosevelt's.

Dudley said he didn't care much for the president. He didn't have any good reason except that Franklin Roosevelt was a Democrat. Evidently that meant he was like the devil himself.

I pointed out that President Roosevelt had done a whole lot to make jobs for people during hard times.

"How would you know?" asked Dudley. "Your father didn't exactly hold down a job."

I heard Janie Aderholt gasp. Like she couldn't believe Dudley would say such a thing about a dead man. Or probably she was feeling sorry for me on account of Pop being who he was.

"I'll have you know that my pop was a farmer," I said. "At least he didn't sell moonshine. Which happens to be against the law."

"The reason your daddy didn't sell moonshine," said

Dudley, "is because he'd have drunk it faster than he could sell it."

I was on my feet then, heading toward the back of the room. But just like that, Miss Hinkle was beside me. She grabbed ahold of my shirtsleeve.

"Sit down, Junior." She said it real low, but there was something in her voice that told me I better listen. Or else.

So I sat. But inside I was standing up. Inside I was marching to the back of the room and jerking that Dudley Catfish Walker up and showing him what a Democrat could do to a Republican. If he wanted a fight, I was of a mind to let him have it.

Miss Hinkle tried to bring the discussion back to the economy and how, if we did go to war, we'd have to sacrifice on more luxuries here at home. That didn't help because Dudley had opinions on that too, and I spoke out and said his ideas were stupid so maybe he should just dry up, and Dudley said I was dumber than a box of rocks.

"That's it," said Miss Hinkle. "The two of you will stay after school."

At the end of the day she told us both to sit in our seats until the buses had gone home. But first she sent notes home to our parents. She asked Janie Aderholt to deliver them down the hall—one to Dudley's brother Rob and one to Ann Fay so she could give it to my momma.

I did not like the thought of Momma getting that

note. And I wasn't crazy about Ann Fay being the one to deliver it, either.

The buses left and Miss Hinkle sent me to the basement to borrow a bucket and mop from the janitor. "Fill it with water and soap," she said. When I came back, Dudley had cleaned the blackboards and Miss Hinkle had him moving all the desks so I could wash the floor.

"Don't you boys dare say a word to each other," said Miss Hinkle. "If you do, you'll find yourselves out of this classroom for the rest of the week. I might just let you sit in the principal's office to do your work."

I mopped every inch of the floor that wasn't covered with heavy furniture. Seemed like she gave me the hard work, mopping and rinsing and wringing the mop out over and over.

But I got some satisfaction out of her sending Dudley outside to dust off the chalkboard erasers. That was almost a girl's job. I could see him smacking them together and sending clouds of dust into the air. Looked like he was talking to himself the whole time. Probably cussing up a blue streak.

When Miss Hinkle was ready to leave, she took us home in her car. We sat in the back seat crowded up against the doors, staring out opposite windows. I wasn't all that mad anymore, so I guessed mopping had worked some of it out of my system. But I was starting to worry about what this would do to Momma.

Miss Hinkle dropped Dudley off first. I had an idea

where he lived, but I hadn't actually ever seen his house. I didn't expect it to be such a shack. I could have made a comment or two about his daddy not fixing the broken-down porch, but I kept my mouth shut. He hopped out of the car and started to walk away.

Miss Hinkle stopped him in his tracks. "Come back here, Dudley."

He turned and came back.

"I believe you forgot to thank me for the ride home."

Dudley squinted at her like his ears couldn't believe what they were hearing. Then he looked away. He rubbed the toe of his shoe in the dirt and stared at the ground. I could tell he didn't want to say thank you. But he finally did. "Thank you, Miss Hinkle."

"That's better."

I told Miss Hinkle I could walk from her house, but no, she wouldn't have that. "I am responsible for you and I will see you to your door." So she drove up our lane and of course Jesse and Butch came out and howled like always until they saw me get out of the car. "Thank you for the ride home, Miss Hinkle," I said.

Momma was waiting for me in the kitchen. "Ann Fay dropped by with a note from Miss Pauline. How could you, Junior? What has gotten into you?"

"What?"

"You were fighting?"

"No."

"That's what the note said."

"We swapped a few words, that's all. Dudley Walker was insulting Pop in front of the class."

"In front of the class?" Momma's eyes narrowed and her voice went from accusing me to disliking Dudley. "What did he say?"

I shouldn't have told her that. Momma didn't need more public shaming. I shrugged. "Nothing, Momma. I'm just hotheaded. That's all."

Momma didn't ask more questions. She probably didn't want to know. I was starting to think I was too much for her to handle. She was used to having Pop there to straighten me out whenever I was ornery.

I never *was* much of a troublemaker, but if I did cause her grief, Pop would say, "You go outside and leave your momma alone." He'd put me to work hoeing weeds or chopping firewood until I was good and sorry for how I'd acted and ready to tell her so.

Granddaddy was standing at the bedroom door listening to me and Momma. Of course he had to throw in his two cents. "Acorn sure don't fall far from the tree."

I knew what he meant. Pop was the tree and I was the acorn that was turning out to be just like him.

Granddaddy shook his finger at Momma. "I'll tell you what's the God's honest truth. Whenever Axel got in trouble at school, he could sure count on double trouble when I got ahold of him. Ten licks at school meant twenty at home."

Momma stared into the gravy she was stirring. And

I could tell she was feeling sorry for Pop—back when he was a boy. "Axel Bledsoe," she said, and she let out a long, ragged-sounding sigh. "God rest your poor tormented soul."

Hearing her fret over Pop just added to my guilt. I didn't like her being disappointed in me. After all, the two of us had always stuck together when he didn't come home or was in one of his dark moods. Now that he wasn't here, it seemed like we were starting to be on opposite sides.

"How many licks did she give you?" Granddaddy headed toward me fingering his belt, like he was fixing to take it off and help Momma out.

"Hammer, you stay out of this," said Momma. "Axel never laid a hand on that child, and I sure won't let you do it."

Granddaddy stopped in his tracks. "It figgers," he said. "Children nowadays are spoiled plumb rotten. Watch and see if you don't regret this."

Since Pop wasn't there to punish me, I figured I'd do it for him. I could show Momma I wasn't trying to be mean and ornery. "I'm gonna chop wood," I told her. "There's a big tree down behind the barn that needs cutting up."

Momma nodded. But she didn't look at me. "I'll call you when supper's ready."

The ax felt real good in my hands. And bringing it down on the log and sending chips flying felt even better. But it didn't take long before I started hankering after

90

that two-man saw hanging on the wall inside the shed.

"Come on, Pop!" I yelled. "You expecting me to do this all by myself? You never did. No siree! You always had me there helping out. So *what* in tarnation makes you think you can run off and leave me here with all the work?"

I wore myself slap out before supper and got only three sections of that log chopped off. Looked like Momma would have to put on extra layers this winter. Or pray for mild weather. Because firewood sure didn't cut itself up, and Granddaddy wouldn't have helped even if he had two good hands.

Pop was right when he said he could stop me from playing baseball. Maybe he wouldn't have let me play if he was still living. But one thing for sure. With him dead, there wasn't a chance of me having time for fun and games.

15

THANKSGIVING
November 1941

Saturday morning before Thanksgiving, I was in the woods just behind the barn chopping away at that log and wishing I was out hunting. But much as Momma would've loved to have some venison to put in jars or squirrel to stew, those things wouldn't keep us warm.

After working for an hour, I threw a few short sections of the log onto the wagon. "Grover," I said, slapping him on the rump, "you might want to catch yourself some shut-eye. This is going to take a while."

I worked for another hour and then I heard voices. Coming around the corner of the barn was Leroy Honeycutt with a two-man saw. Of course Ann Fay was with him.

She ran ahead, waving a newspaper. "Look, Junior. Somebody famous was in town this week. Alvin York. He's a war hero. They made a movie about him."

"I know that," I said. "I heard about the movie on the radio."

"Well, he stayed at Hotel Hickory last week—on his

way to Statesville for a movie premiere. I bet you know all about that too, don't you?"

"Nope," I said. "Don't know much about Hollywood."

"Peggy Sue says a premiere is the first showing of the movie. When *Sergeant York* comes to Hickory, me and Peggy Sue are going to see it."

That figured. Her and Peggy Sue. "Well, y'all have yourself a good time," I said.

"Wanna go? I bet her momma'll take you too."

Of course I wanted to go. And Mildred probably *would* take me. But I sure didn't want to be beholden to anybody. So I just shook my head. "I don't have time for picture shows. I'll be cutting firewood every Saturday between now and Christmas."

"We're here to help with that," said Leroy. "You got right smart of a load there, Junior. But the biggest part of that tree is still on the ground. We best get to work."

Well, I could just hardly believe I had help. Things went a lot faster with me and Leroy using the crosscut saw. Ann Fay climbed onto the wagon and started stacking the sections I'd already loaded—even the hefty logs that still needed to be split. If she couldn't pick it up, she'd roll or shove it into place. I'll say one thing for that young'un. She sure knew how to work.

By noon we had a wagonload. "Ready to take this back to the house?" asked Leroy. "We should head home, and I 'spect you've worked up an appetite."

We led Grover back to the house and unhitched him

by the chopping block in the backyard. "I sure do thank you both," I said. "Maybe Momma will rest easy now that we have a good start on the firewood."

Of course I still had to split it, but I could do that, a little at a time, on weekdays after school.

Granddaddy was waiting for me at the back door. "Where you been? I need a haircut. And my toenails have to be trimmed."

I guessed he thought I was actually going to trim his toenails! But he was sure wrong about that. Momma had dinner dished up and I sat down to eat.

Granddaddy tagged along. "Mind if I join you? After dinner we'll get right on that haircut. And then maybe I'll take me a bath. I could use one."

I could've agreed about him needing a bath. As usual he had tobacco stains running down his neck. But ignoring him was my best bet.

"Hammer, I already filled you a plate," said Momma. "It's in your room."

"Can you bring it here?"

"I could," said Momma. "But then what would you do?" She waited for Granddaddy to leave the table, and then she sat down. "Miss Dinah came by," she said to me. "It looks like we have an invitation for Thanksgiving."

I dropped my fork. "You made plans to go to the Hinkle sisters', Momma? I can't! I put up with Miss Pauline five days a week already."

Momma squinted. "You need to climb down off your high horse. Nobody said a thing about having Thanksgiving at the Hinkle sisters'. Your Uncle Tag called to invite us to China Grove for a few days. Miss Dinah just delivered the message. If you can arrange for milking and someone to tend to the animals, we'll do it."

"Garland Abernethy will help with the animals," I said. Garland's farm was only a mile away, and he and Pop often helped each other out when one of them was away from home. We used to go regular to China Grove for Thanksgiving or Christmas, but the last few years it seemed like Pop ended up drunk around any holiday. Momma wouldn't visit her family if he was intoxicated. Or "sick," as she always called it.

Before I had time to get used to the idea of leaving for a few days, I heard Granddaddy coming up behind me. Singing. "*Over the river and through the woods, to Grandmother's house we go . . .*" He plopped his plate on the table, pulled out Pop's chair, and sat beside me. "Yipee!" he said. "We're going out of town. Yup, I'm definitely going to need a haircut."

I looked at Momma. She was sitting there staring at her plate. Ignoring him. I hoped she knew that if she intended on taking him to China Grove, I would stay home and enjoy every minute of peace and quiet.

"I'll give you a haircut after we eat," Momma told Granddaddy. "And I'll trim your nails."

I slid my chair back from the table. "I'm staying home," I said. And then I headed to the back porch with my dinner.

"Stop right there." That was Momma talking, her voice cold as November. "What did I tell you about that high horse?"

I turned. Granddaddy was grinning. Just waiting for her to bless me out.

Momma pointed her fork at him. "Junior and I will go to China Grove with my brother. If *you* want to celebrate Thanksgiving with family, Tag will drop you off in Brookford on our way out of town."

Granddaddy speared a few beans with his fork and waved it in the air. "Hot dog! That is a crackerjack idea. Won't Lucy and Lily be surprised!"

For the first time since Granddaddy arrived, all three of us were excited about the very same thing.

On Thanksgiving morning Granddaddy was sitting on the porch waiting for Uncle Tag. He climbed into the front seat and told Tag how fast to drive and where to turn toward Brookford.

The aunts' two white houses were like twins standing side by side, practically up against the street. Stepping-stones curved from the driveways to their porches. But Granddaddy didn't take either one of those paths. He trotted between their houses and stood there looking in one direction and then the other like he couldn't decide which back door to sneak up on. Aunt Lucille's front door opened and she popped her head out just as Uncle Tag backed out the driveway.

I got a chuckle out of that. So did Momma, who had moved up to the front seat. "Lucille, honey," she said, "you don't know what just hit you."

By nine-thirty we were in China Grove. The two-story house where my grandparents lived had ivy growing up the walls. Somebody kept it trimmed back real neat around the windows. There was a porch that went around three sides of the house. I remembered speeding on a big tricycle from one end of that porch to the other. When we drove up, two little cousins I didn't recognize were using the trike, one of them standing on the back. "That's Vinnie doing the pedaling," said Uncle Tag. "And his sister Rita behind him."

Uncle Tag's wife, Evalona, grabbed me and kissed both of my cheeks. "Bless your heart, Bessie," she said. "The boy's all grown up. Next thing, he'll be out gallivanting. Better keep your eye on him."

"No," said Momma. "Junior never gives me a minute's trouble."

We sat down to the grandest feast I'd ever seen. I figured President Roosevelt had a bigger turkey, but I bet his pies weren't as good as ours. And how could he have a family that was as warm and loving as Momma's? Gramps told stories from the Great War, and Uncle Tag said how Momma used to feed him mud pies with blackberries—back when she was five and he was four.

It felt strange to be sitting there like that, stuffing myself with food and good feelings. Never once had I sat at a table with Pop's family and listened to stories about him growing up.

It was a warm day, so after dinner the grown-ups, who were feeling fat and lazy, sat around on the front porch watching the children do somersaults and spin themselves in circles. Little Vinnie spun himself dizzy and staggered around the yard—just being goofy. "Look at me," he said. "I'm drunk. I'm Axel Bledsoe."

"You hush, Vinnie," said Uncle Tag.

But it was too late. I'd already heard it and Momma did too. Silence fell across that porch full of relatives. Somebody had some explaining to do; because that young'un never even knew my pop.

"How would he know to say a thing like that?" asked Momma.

"Um, uh." Gramps stuttered around, trying to come up with something to smooth things over.

Finally Uncle Tag spoke up. "Vinnie must have overheard the story about Axel getting intoxicated a few years back. At Junior's birthday dinner."

"And I wonder who passed that story down the line?" said Momma. "Since Vinnie was just a baby when that happened. Apparently this isn't the first time you've been entertained at the expense of my husband's reputation. Have you no respect?"

I knew what Momma was saying because I had that

feeling too. That if we hadn't been there, everybody would've thought little Vinnie was real cute.

"Maybe we won't stay overnight after all," said Momma. "Tag, would you please take us home?"

So much for getting two days away. So much for having a good time with Momma's family. So much for having any family at all. It seemed like one way or another Pop was always getting in the way of me and family.

Granny and Gramps tried to put their arms around Momma and tell her how sorry they were and how nobody meant her any harm. But she wouldn't listen to them. I didn't know when I'd seen Momma so mad. Not even Granddaddy could rile her up the way her own family could.

I don't think she said another word to any one of them until we were in the car with Uncle Tag. "You people never did like Axel," she said.

"We liked him fine," said Uncle Tag. "When he wasn't drinking. Maybe you should've left him and come back home to live. Now that he's gone, there's nothing to keep you in Hickory. Why not move to China Grove?"

Nothing to keep us in Hickory? What did he think? That we could walk away from our life there? Our neighbors? And the house we lived in with Pop?

"No," said Momma. "I couldn't. I have Axel's father to care for." But she wasn't fooling anybody.

It was like her family had just fired a shot at us. And

if they wanted a fight, she would let them have it.

I had felt so thankful at dinner, surrounded by relatives who didn't fight. But it looked like I was wrong about Momma's family. Maybe they weren't all that different from the Bledsoes. I felt confused. I wanted Momma's family, but right that minute, if God was to give me a choice between the two, I'd ask for Pop back— in a heartbeat.

Momma kept her eyes straight ahead and her shoulders stiff as laundry frozen on the wash line. Uncle Tag gave up talking and started fiddling with the knob on his radio. The radio was saying that President Roosevelt did not have turkey and dressing with polio sufferers in Warm Springs, Georgia, like he usually did. Instead he was in Washington trying to keep us from going to war with the Japanese.

There were lights on in the house when Uncle Tag dropped us off. And Granddaddy was in the kitchen with a plateful of leftovers. It looked like when he took a notion, he could heat food for himself.

Momma just stared at him, and I could see tears spilling out of her eyes. After what she'd been through that day, Granddaddy was the straw that was fixing to break the camel's back. "I thought you were in Brookford," she said.

"Hee hee," said Granddaddy. "I reckon I wore out my welcome."

That figured. Granddaddy had made his own

young'uns so miserable they didn't last a day with him. So what did they do? Dumped him back on us. And we would just stand by and take it. What else *could* we do? Turn him out in the cold?

Nothing made sense to me anymore. Especially not family. Not Pop's family, not Momma's either. Why couldn't people just get along in this world? That's what I wanted to know.

16

WAR!
December 1941

"Dadgummit," I said. "What does diagramming sentences have to do with life?" The world could be coming to an end and Miss Hinkle still expected me to spend Sunday afternoon figuring out this nonsense. Maybe Pop was right about book learning. But Pop's opinion didn't count much anymore, since he was dead.

Now, *there* was a sentence I could diagram. *My pop is dead.* But what was the point of breaking something like that apart and putting the words on crazy lines going this way and that? It sure didn't help me feel better, and it didn't bring him back either. Still, for some reason I wrote that sentence down. Maybe if I put *that* in a diagram Miss Hinkle would see how useless this assignment was.

I started drawing lines. I knew *pop* was the subject and I knew *my* described Pop, so that meant it was an adjective. I knew *is* was the predicate. But what was *dead*? Where did it belong in that stupid diagram?

Right in the middle of me trying to figure that out, Granddaddy let out a big whoop on the other side of the bedroom door. And just like that he flung the door open and yelled, "War! The Japs started it. I knew they would. I told you so. Finally we're going to war."

He was so excited you'd think the president himself had announced it. But I knew that Granddaddy declaring war didn't mean it was so.

"Git in here!" Granddaddy waved me toward him. I pulled a kitchen chair close to the door and sat just outside the room. Momma, who'd been napping in her bedroom, heard all the commotion and pulled up another chair. The radio announcer said that Pearl Harbor had been bombed.

"What's Pearl Harbor?" asked Momma.

"Naval base. Hi-wah-ee." Granddaddy turned the volume as high as he could. The radio announcer's voice was deep, and every line of it sounded like a worse threat than the one before. "*A Japanese attack upon Pearl Harbor* naturally *would mean war. Such an attack would* naturally *bring a counter attack. And hostilities of this kind would* naturally *mean that the president would ask Congress for a declaration of war.*"

I was used to Granddaddy announcing war. But hearing that man's serious-sounding voice, piling one argument on top of another, was a whole different story. All of a sudden it felt like the bombs could start dropping right here in the United States.

And if they did, where in the world would we go? It wasn't like we had a basement to hide in.

103

"Lord, have mercy." Momma sank back in her chair. Then she grabbed my arm. "Thank God you're too young to fight."

But I wasn't too young to fight. Gideon Bledsoe was staring at me from across the room. Wasn't he close to my age when he fought in the Civil War? And hadn't Pop taught me how to aim? I didn't say any of that to Momma, though.

We spent most of that Sunday listening to the commentators predicting that we'd automatically be at war with Japan's allies—Germany and Italy.

After a while I couldn't take the worry anymore, so I went outside. The cold air smelled of wood smoke from people's chimneys. The colored church was having a meeting and I heard them singing. "*Nobody knows the trouble I've seen.*"

That was for sure.

I went to the barn. "Come on, Grover," I said. "Let's go for a ride." I turned him toward Bakers Mountain. I wondered where Frank Jenkins was by now. It appeared he'd soon be fighting. It felt good knowing I had boosted his morale with that BB gun Pop gave me.

I never did finish my homework. I turned in that one sentence and Miss Hinkle frowned and handed it back to me. "What happened, Junior?"

"The war," I said. "I couldn't think."

"There is no war," said Miss Hinkle. But her voice

wobbled a tiny bit, and I was pretty sure she didn't believe her own self.

The principal, Mr. Hollar, came on the loudspeaker. "Teachers, I want you to bring your students to the auditorium for a special announcement from the president of the United States. You have fifteen minutes to assemble."

Never mind that Miss Hinkle was the strictest teacher in the school. Never mind that she was clapping her hands to get our attention. Seemed like everybody in the room was talking out loud, some of us to ourselves and some to the person beside us. Janie Aderholt dropped her head into her arms. I heard Marilyn Overcash say, "Oh dear God, we're going to war. And my uncle just got drafted. Dear God, no!"

Miss Hinkle clapped her hands again. "Class! Be quiet!"

But we didn't settle down, so she grabbed the yardstick out of the chalk tray under the blackboard. And slammed it hard across her desk.

Janie yelped and leaped out of her chair. And everyone else went dead silent. Janie looked around and then, realizing that everyone was staring at her, sat down. Fast. Her shoulders were heaving, and I heard her trying to catch her breath.

"You may put down your pencils and papers," said Miss Hinkle—as if any of us were actually practicing the handwriting exercise for the day. She pointed to the sentence on the board—*Union of interests brings union of minds.*

"The bombing of Pearl Harbor is something that unites us with other countries that have also been senselessly attacked. Now you may go single file to the auditorium to hear what the president has to say about this. No talking, please."

No talking? That was impossible. We all poured into the auditorium, and the only ones not talking were the ones who were too scared to open their mouths. But when President Roosevelt came on the radio every sound in the room just dribbled away. First there was a crackling noise, and then the president's voice came at us from the big brown speaker boxes at both sides of the stage. "*Yesterday, December 7, 1941—a date which will live in infamy—the United States of America was suddenly and deliberately attacked by naval and air forces of the Empire of Japan.*"

The president told how Japan was pretending to hold peace talks with the United States, but obviously they'd been planning this attack all along. "*I regret to tell you that very many American lives have been lost.*"

He named all the other places that Japan had attacked. Malaya. Hong Kong, Guam, the Philippine Islands. Wake Island and Midway Island. They'd bombed seven places in one day. Seven places that were minding their own business, trying to live in peace.

President Roosevelt said he was asking Congress to declare war with the Japanese Empire. Then his voice went away, and all I heard was wooden auditorium chairs creaking, shoes scuffling against the floor, and here and there somebody crying.

Mr. Hollar stood up. "Yes," he said, "America is in danger, but we must keep our wits about us. We will all be needed in one way or another to help our country's struggle for freedom."

Beside me, Janie was chewing her fingernails. And I heard somebody cracking their knuckles. I looked down at my hands and realized that while the president was talking, I had crumpled my homework paper into a wrinkled wad. I didn't even remember carrying it into the auditorium.

. . .

On Tuesday night President Roosevelt addressed the nation again. Right before he came on, there was a knock at the back door. When I opened it, Leroy and Ann Fay were standing there.

"We came to hear the president," said Ann Fay.

Leroy put his hand on her shoulder. "If your grandfather doesn't mind."

"And so what if Hammer does mind?" said Momma. "This is my house."

She headed toward the bedroom door. Granddaddy was right there waiting. And obviously he'd been listening.

"The more the merrier," he said. As if war was some kind of party he was throwing. He reached for his can of Skoal and screwed off the lid. "Pull up a chair." He dipped his thumb and finger into the tobacco and stuffed the wad behind his lower lip.

Leroy brought chairs to the bedroom door, and we crowded together in a half circle to listen. Of course, Granddaddy sat in his rocking chair inside the room, controlling the radio. You would think he was the president himself, the way he held his head so high and welcomed the neighbors in. Then, all of a sudden, he hushed everyone and turned up the volume.

President Roosevelt started speaking. "*Powerful and resourceful gangsters have banded together to make war upon the whole human race,*" he said. He listed all the places that Japan, Italy, and Germany had attacked, and every time he named a place he said *without warning.*

Now they were after us. The way he laid it all out, you could almost feel the enemy coming down the lane.

The house creaked. It was only the wind, but Ann Fay jumped. She was already clinging to Leroy's arm, but she slid off her chair and he pulled her close. She leaned into him, staring at the radio and biting her lip to keep from crying. He wrapped his arms around her and leaned his head against hers and they listened like that, hanging on to each other.

"*We are now in this war,*" said the president. "*We are all in it—all the way. Every single man, woman, and child is a partner in the most tremendous undertaking of our American history.*"

Momma's hands kept busy the whole time. Her knitting needles clicked against each other as she worked out her nervousness, making another pair of socks to go overseas to some soldier.

"*So we are going to win the war,*" said President Roosevelt, "*and we are going to win the peace that follows.*"

Granddaddy's rocking chair was still going, slow and steady for a change—like someone had wound it up and now it kept the pace that was set for it. For once, it was like the old man had run out of opinions; he wasn't disagreeing with anything the president said. He just stared across the room at his daddy's picture. Tobacco juice leaked out the corner of his mouth, but evidently he wasn't noticing he needed to spit.

A war will grow you right up, Granddaddy had said when he showed me Gideon's portrait.

That picture of my great-granddaddy made me realize war could do a lot of things. It could win us our peace and make the world a safe place to live. We all wanted that. But it could make a hardness too.

And like the president said, we were now in it. All the way.

17

SERGEANT YORK
December 1941

Christmas never seemed as sentimental to Momma and me as it did to everybody else. But everybody else didn't have a pop who, like as not, was often sprawled across the bed on Christmas Day, sleeping off his whiskey.

This year was worse than most. This year we knew for sure we wouldn't see him at all, sober or drunk. This year America was at war. And Granddaddy was here.

Maybe I didn't understand Pop and moonshine, but I found out real quick that being around Granddaddy at Christmas was enough to drive anybody to drink. He sang at the top of his lungs whenever he took a notion, making fun of Christmas cheer. Sometimes he'd throw in an extra line or two of his own just to show how cantankerous he was feeling.

To make things even worse, Granddaddy heard on the radio one Saturday morning that Russell Crump from Brookford was killed at Pearl Harbor. "Give me that picture," he said, pointing to one of his newspaper clippings on the wall.

When I handed it over—lo and behold, there were tears in Granddaddy's eyes.

His hand trembled, making Russell's picture shake. "Inez used to feed that freckled face," he said in a voice that was kind of wobbly. "He'd come hanging on to our porch post, looking like a little lost orphan. 'I smell liver mush,' he'd say. Or, 'My momma don't got no food in the house.'" Granddaddy ran his stub over Russell's picture real gentle-like. "He had a pitiful little way about him. And my Inez—God rest her soul—she never could say no to him."

Was I dreaming or was this Hammer Bledsoe? If Granddaddy could care that way about a neighbor boy, why wasn't he the least bit sad about his own son dying? If Pop had died in battle instead of by the side of the road, would Granddaddy be shedding tears for him?

And what about me? I was his grandson, for Pete's sake. Maybe he would give a hoot about me too, if I was old enough to join the army. Would that earn his respect? As it was, I was just someone to boss around and remind him of Pop. And he hated Pop.

He was so intent on that picture of Russell Crump that I doubt he even noticed when I slipped out. The stack of firewood on the back porch was shrinking fast, and I had to work on it or Momma would be fussing.

It was a relief to be outside, breathing cold, clean air. Off in the distance I heard a woodpecker working away on a tree too.

While I was chopping wood, cars started showing up—women from Momma's sewing circle. They used to quilt or mend clothes, but nowadays they put together first-aid kits for the Red Cross. Or knitted socks for soldiers.

They went in the front door and I stayed in the backyard, trying to keep out of their way.

I had everything I needed out there. Well water for drinking. The outhouse for other business. And peace and quiet from Granddaddy.

A couple of hours later, when the women started leaving, Mildred Rhinehart came out the back door. "Good morning, Junior."

"Morning, Mildred." I laid my ax by the woodpile and went to the porch to see what she wanted.

"I'm taking Peggy Sue and Ann Fay to see *Sergeant York* this afternoon. Would you like to go along?"

Sergeant York? I could actually see that movie? "I sure would. Thank you very much. If Momma agrees, that is."

"She's already agreed," said Mildred. "The movie will be my treat."

Mildred probably thought I didn't have fifteen cents to my name. Truth was, me and Momma needed every penny we had, but I didn't want a handout. "Oh, no," I said. "That's mighty nice of you. But I have money."

Mildred shook her head. "I insist on buying your ticket."

112

"Well, I'll pay you back," I said. "Have any work I can do?"

Mildred swatted her hand in the air to let me know the discussion was closed.

I carried water to the woodstove to heat for a bath. Then I set the privacy screen by the stove and soaked in soapy water. It wouldn't do to have Peggy Sue and Ann Fay holding their noses over the smell of my armpits.

Granddaddy watched me comb my hair down in front of the bedroom mirror. "Where you going in your glad rags on a Saturday afternoon?"

"To the picture show," I said.

"And sit there watching lovers quarrel when there's a war on? What's this world coming to?"

"I don't know, sir—an end, maybe. That's what Reverend Price keeps preaching. He says with all the wickedness the Germans and the Italians and the Japs are doing, the world is bound to be coming to an end."

Outside, Jesse and Butch started yapping and Mildred tooted her car horn. "Sorry, Granddaddy. I gotta go."

The movie started off with a bang—actually, with a whole lot of bangs, because Alvin York was riding his horse around outside a church building and shooting his gun like crazy in the middle of the singing and preaching. York had a God-fearing momma inside that church who was mighty embarrassed by his shenanigans.

But then he got religion. His religion was against moonshine, card playing, and raising heck. So he gave all that up. It was against killing too, but Uncle Sam drafted him into the Great War. Since he didn't have a choice, he used his sharpshooting skills to capture a passel of Germans and he came home a hero, with a huge parade in New York City.

That movie coming out right then—I knew it was somebody's way of trying to work up our patriotism. After all, lots of people were being drafted. Sergeant York's story was intended to make all of us want to fight the Germans.

When I got home, I set up a pasteboard target on the side of Pop's shed. Seeing Sergeant York shoot made me want to practice my aim. Only problem was, when I went for the BB gun I remembered I'd given all my BBs away during the army maneuvers.

I sat on the sweet potato crate and ran my hands over that gun. It was one of those surprises Pop showed up with for no reason at all—one day, back when I was seven and he had a good year working at the cotton gin over in Blackburn.

Those were the days when I tagged along after him like Ann Fay after Leroy. Back then he put up that porch swing so the three of us could sit there on Sunday evenings.

We'd listen to the sound of the colored choir singing in the church next door. Daddy would sing along. "*I'm just a poor wayfaring stranger, traveling through this world of woe, yet there's no sickness, toil, nor danger in that bright land to which I go . . ."*

I hoped he was happy in that bright land. Because one thing for sure—this world he left behind was full of woe.

18

CHRISTMAS
December 1941

The newspapers and radio were asking people to cut down on travel over Christmas. That way we'd be saving gasoline for the war effort. But Uncle Tag called and suggested we take the train to China Grove. Momma sent me to the Hinkle sisters' house to call him back.

"I'm sorry we can't come," I told him. "Momma feels uneasy with the war on. She wants to stick close to home."

Uncle Tag was quiet for a minute. "Maybe next year, then." I could hear in his voice that he knew her real reason. "I'm sorry about what happened at Thanksgiving," he said.

"I know. Maybe next year Momma will be over it." I hoped she would. I remembered spending Christmas with Momma's people back before Pop started drinking. I wasn't ready to give up on them, even if I was offended by Vinnie acting drunk like Axel Bledsoe.

Because of the gasoline situation, the Honeycutts decided not to visit Ann Fay's Mamaw and Papaw in

Georgia. So Momma invited them to eat Christmas dinner with us.

Come Christmas morning, Granddaddy was singing before he lifted his head off the pillow. "*God rest ye merry gentlemen . . .*" I sure wished I could load him in a car and drive him over to Brookford. Why couldn't the aunts take their father off our hands for one day out of the year?

The Honeycutts showed up at twelve o'clock noon. Driving up the lane right behind them was Miss Pauline's Plymouth.

"Momma! You didn't invite the Hinkle sisters?"

"They're our neighbors too."

"And Miss Hinkle is my teacher."

"She won't be giving quizzes today."

It was too late for me to argue. In no time the house was filled with neighbors. I carried everybody's coats to Momma's bed. I almost never went into her room. It had always seemed like a private place just for her and Pop. But now I wanted to stay there in that quiet space. It wasn't anything fancy, but the quilt on her bed and the curtains she'd made for the windows made it seem like something almost grand. Her sewing machine sat there waiting for Christmas to be over so she could go back to working on clothes she was making for the Red Cross to give to soldiers' families.

There was a bureau with a side of drawers for Momma and one for Pop. I slid open Pop's top drawer.

His handkerchiefs were there, folded into squares, large blue ones for weekdays and smaller white ones for Sundays. Momma kept his socks and his drawers in neat piles too. And there was a cigar there. Pop didn't smoke much, except when he was out playing poker. And then he most always came home drunk.

I picked up that cigar and breathed in sweet, cherry-smelling sorrow. It hit me so hard I hung on to the bureau to steady myself. When I looked at their bed, I could almost see him stretched across it with his mouth hanging open. And Momma sitting beside him, running her fingers through his hair. Praying. But praying hadn't done her any good, had it?

Why, God? That's what I wanted to know. *Why didn't you answer her prayers? Wasn't Bessie Bledsoe good enough? Or was it me that was so bad?*

"Junior." Momma was calling me for dinner.

"Coming." I put the cigar back, just the way I found it in the front of the drawer. Right that minute I didn't feel like eating turkey with my neighbors. Especially Miss Hinkle. But I couldn't exactly get out of it either.

By the time I got to the kitchen, Momma was sitting people to the table, and I heard Granddaddy starting up a song. "*Good King Wenceslas looked out, on the feast of Stephen.*"

He stood at the bedroom door staring at the feast Momma had cooked up. He'd combed his hair for a change and was even wearing a necktie. I didn't even know he owned such a thing. When he saw me heading for the table Granddaddy hurried over and plopped himself down in the only chair that was left. Mine. And not only that, it was right beside Miss Pauline. "Looks like it's going to be a mighty fine Christmas," he said. "Pretty women and everthing."

Miss Pauline gave him a look. "*Every*thing," she said. "Not *ever*thing."

Granddaddy laughed. "You're that mean teacher I been hearing about."

Everybody in the room went real quiet—except Ida and Ellie and baby Bobby, because they didn't know enough to be embarrassed for me. I felt my face turning red as a candy cane. "Miss Hinkle, I never said that. Granddaddy, I was fixing to bring a plate of food to your room."

"Not unless the pretty lady comes too."

Well, you should have seen Miss Pauline's face when he said that. Now she was the one turning red. Miss Dinah started to snicker, but Miss Pauline gave her a look that would erase the chalk right off a blackboard.

I knew Momma wanted Granddaddy to go back in that room and shut the door, but she wasn't about to make a scene in front of the neighbors. She got up from the table. "Take my seat," she told me. "I'll be busy serving. Let's bless the food."

Just like that, Granddaddy started thanking God, almost like he believed what he was saying. But I knew he was putting on a show for the pretty ladies.

I was supposed to have my eyes shut, but instead I was studying Miss Pauline, thinking *What's so pretty?* If you asked me, Miss Dinah was better looking than she was. But they both looked old to me. Maybe older than Granddaddy.

Soon as Granddaddy finished saying grace, he started bothering Miss Pauline. "How's the boy doing at school? I betcha he's a holy terror." He bumped my elbow and laughed.

"Holy terror," said Miss Pauline. "I'm quite certain that is an oxymoron."

Granddaddy was buttering a biscuit, but he stopped with his knife in midair. "A what kind of moron?"

I think Miss Pauline chuckled just a little when he said that. "Junior," she said, "tell your grandfather what an oxymoron is."

Was I supposed to know what that was? I racked my brain but couldn't find an oxymoron in there anywhere. "Uh, Miss Hinkle, Momma said you wouldn't be giving any quizzes today."

But Granddaddy wasn't interested anyway. He started going on about Japan taking over the Philippines. "There goes our rubber supply," he said. "There won't be no new tires for your fancy cars. People will have to walk again, the way I did when I was growing up. I never owned a car in my life. Didn't hurt me none."

He filled our ears with war news. I think everybody at the table tried to change the subject at one time or another, but he always brought it back around to war. When Momma was fixing to serve pumpkin pie, Granddaddy looked at Leroy. "Mr. Honeycutt, next thing you know, they'll be moving the draft age. Calling you up."

Ann Fay's eyes went big and round as Momma's pies.

"No, Granddaddy," I said. "He's a married man, and married men aren't being called."

"They done changed that law," said Granddaddy. "Too many young people getting hitched in a hurry so they wouldn't have to serve. That don't work anymore."

"*Doesn't*," said Miss Pauline.

"Dozen?" Granddaddy looked confused. "More than a dozen. Hundreds are hitching up, just to keep out of the draft. Sorry devils."

"*Doesn't* work," said Miss Pauline. "Not *don't* work."

Granddaddy elbowed Miss Pauline. "You're sure itchin' to teach me a thing or two, ain'tcha?"

Miss Pauline scooted herself away from Granddaddy until she was practically sitting on her sister's lap. And she didn't bother to tell him that *ain't* wasn't a real word.

Miss Dinah giggled. "I think he likes you," she whispered.

I was sure having a good time watching Miss Pauline squirm. Too bad Granddaddy couldn't be in her classroom. I'd have liked to be a fly on the wall watching her teach him perfect handwriting. How would she teach Granddaddy, who didn't even have a right hand? And what would the people who wrote *The Palmer Method of Business Writing* say about a person like that?

Maybe they thought Granddaddy didn't have any business trying to write in the first place. Probably somebody like him was expected to stay at home where other people didn't have to see his messed-up arm. And what would that feel like?

I'd never really considered how Granddaddy felt before. But then, I didn't know much at all about him. And I wasn't likely to start asking him questions.

After dinner the women cleaned up the dishes and the twins played with their Christmas presents—paper dolls. Ann Fay wanted to know what I got.

"BBs, for one thing," I said. After she heard that, Ann Fay didn't care about any other presents. She wanted to practice shooting. Leroy said she could target-practice, so I set up a tin can on the fence post and showed her how to hit it every time.

Ann Fay's aim was okay. But mine was a whole lot better. And that right there made me look like a hero in one person's eyes at least.

19

NEW YEAR
January 1942

If there was one thing Miss Hinkle was dead serious about, it was writing. Handwriting and writing essays. She believed that communication was the passport to success. The first handwriting drill for the New Year was:

Good business writing is in demand.
Pull push and practice penmanship.

After we worked on those, Miss Hinkle passed a cigar box around the room, telling us to reach in and choose one of the folded papers with topics written on them.

I drew Woodrow Wilson. What I knew about him I could write in three sentences. *He was our president during the Great War. He was a Democrat. He wore glasses.* Well, actually, I decided I could write another sentence. *Granddaddy hates him.*

Miss Hinkle gave us time to work in class, using magazines and some books and encyclopedias on the shelves under the windows.

The encyclopedias were right there beside my desk, so I grabbed the *W* one. Before I was finished reading about President Wilson, Dudley was beside me. "You got the *W*?" he demanded. "I need it."

"Sorry, pal."

"I'm not your pal. And I want that book."

I knew I wasn't his pal. And I didn't want to be, either. But I knew how to get his goat. "How do I know you even need this encyclopedia, *Catfish*? Maybe you're just trying to start something."

"Maybe I am." Dudley pulled a slip of paper out of his pocket and held it in front of my face—so close I'd have to be cross-eyed to read it. "It says Wilbur Wright—in case you can't read. And don't call me Catfish."

I shrugged. "I might be finished in a minute or two."

"What if I don't have a minute or two? My paper is due the same time as yours."

I started to tell him to find a magazine or one of those other books on the shelf. But then Janie Aderholt, in front of me, turned and said, "Leave him alone, Dudley. When Junior's finished, I'll bring it to you."

Dudley's glare changed into a slow smile. "Well, okay then," he said. "I'll see *you* in a minute or two, Janie dear." He looked at me and smirked as though he had just won a fistfight. He leaned in and lowered his voice. "Got yourself a girl to protect you?" He winked. "Or maybe she's looking after me."

I guess he thought Janie was sweet on him, but when

he walked away, she turned to me and rolled her eyes. "Good riddance," she whispered. We both laughed, and I noticed then that she had some real cute dimples. Funny how I never paid attention to that before.

I wrote a few notes about Woodrow Wilson. He was born in Virginia in 1856, and later he even lived in North Carolina. He was religious. He tried to keep America out of the Great War. And he started the League of Nations, which was supposed to stop the world from ever having a war again.

So how had we landed right in the middle of another one? That's what I wanted to know.

I heard Dudley making noises in the back of the room, so I decided to give up the W encyclopedia. Janie was bent over her page, busy taking notes on whatever her topic was. I tapped her on the shoulder with my pencil. "I'm done for now. In case you want to take this to you know who."

She turned and smiled at me, and I decided that those dimples of hers might just be the best part about coming to school. "What are you writing about?" I asked—hoping she wouldn't notice that I was feeling kind of swoony.

"Infantile paralysis. Polio." She held up the copy of *Time* magazine that she was taking notes from. "It's scary. Any of us could catch it. Even President Roosevelt had it."

I knew that. I figured most people did, because of the

President's Birthday Balls coming up in just a few weeks. Every January there were big fundraiser parties all over the country. Rich people went to the balls, and all the money they gave supported the war against polio. The rest of us just read about it in the newspaper or brought dimes to school to help in our own small way.

Janie reached for the W encyclopedia. "I'll be back," she said. And something about the way she said that made it sound like a promise.

20

PLAYING HOOKY
January 1942

I should have kept that W encyclopedia longer and taken more notes on President Wilson. But at least I'd stayed out of trouble with Dudley, and Momma would've been proud of me for that.

Now I had to write the paper. At home, while I was struggling over it, I came up with the crazy idea to ask Granddaddy for help. If anybody had an opinion on Woodrow Wilson, it was him.

I took my composition book and my pencil into the bedroom. "I have to write a paper."

From the look he gave me, you'd think I'd just told him I was fixing to take his radio away. "Do it someplace else," he said, as if I was an intruder in my own bedroom.

"On Woodrow Wilson."

Granddaddy turned off the radio. "Sit down." He leaned over and spit tobacco juice into the tin can on the floor. Then he wiped his mouth with his stub, leaving it streaked with black.

I pulled a chair in from the kitchen, and by the time

I came back he had that rocker going fifty miles an hour. Before I could ask the first question he started talking. "Wilson was a yellow-livered Democrat. He waited until America was attacked to do a thing about that war. By then it was too late."

"Too late? Why was it too late? I mean, we helped win the war."

Granddaddy shook his head.

"Too late for what?"

He didn't answer me. Matter of fact, I don't think he was even seeing me anymore. The chair stopped rocking. His eyes went cold and hard, and he raised his left arm like he was holding a gun. He steadied it with his right stub. And then he started yanking that trigger finger. "Axel. You sorry little upstart." His voice dropped real low and mean. "It was all your fault."

Axel? Pop? What did he mean, it was Pop's fault? "Granddaddy! What are you talking about?"

Evidently Granddaddy remembered where he was then. He dropped his arms and pounded the arm of the rocking chair. Then he said, "Go on. Git outta here." He shut his eyes and clamped his teeth, but that trigger finger on his left hand kept on jerking.

I don't know why I let him run me out of my own room. Except it didn't much feel like mine anymore, and that room with him in it was scary sometimes. I needed some outside air.

I pulled on my coat and hat with the flaps that

fit down over the ears and headed out the back door. Butch and Jesse hurried to meet me. I stopped on the big stone step and gave them each a good belly scratch. Then I stuffed my hands in my pockets and took off walking, out past the oak tree and the shed until I came to the garden. It was a tangle of dead vines and a few bent corn stalks—dark as shadows against the earth.

Pop would have loved this night. The air was crispy cold, and the stars were so bright they put me in mind of millions of headlights off in the distance. I sure wished they could shine some light on my understanding.

"Pop? He said it was all your fault. What was all your fault? What did you do? And why was he acting like he wanted to shoot somebody?"

There was a whole lot I didn't understand about Granddaddy. But I was starting to realize something. Whatever was wrong with my pop was probably Granddaddy's fault. Instead of the other way around. When Pop was alive I was busy just trying to get *him* to notice *me*. It never crossed my mind to ask questions about *him*. Now I wished I had.

After a while I heard Momma on the back porch, banging the water dipper against the well bucket and calling my name.

"Coming, Momma."

She was waiting in the kitchen with a cup of hot Postum. "Child, it's freezing out there. Land sakes! I thought you fell through the hole in the outhouse."

"I was just having a little talk with Pop. That's all."

"Oh," said Momma. "And what did he have to say?"

I shrugged. "Nothing much."

During the night I dreamed about Granddaddy standing in the middle of Brookford pointing a gun at Pop. He was yanking that trigger finger. And I just knew my pop was about to die.

I woke up with one big question. *Why did Granddaddy hate his own young'un so much?*

I headed off to school that morning without finishing that paper on Woodrow Wilson. Every time I thought about it, my mind went back to Granddaddy and how he went from talking about President Wilson to my pop. What in the world did they have to do with each other?

When the bus turned in to the school I could see where the highway made a sharp turn toward Hickory. At the bottom of that hill on the way into town was Brookford. My aunts, who were too sorry to take care of their own daddy, were less than a half mile away from me right that minute.

All of a sudden I wanted to talk to them. Maybe I could learn some things. So, just like that, I decided to pay a visit to Pop's sisters.

I waited until last to get off the bus. When the rest of the students went through the side door of the school, I moseyed over to the front of the school grounds past Miss Hinkle's Plymouth and all the other teachers' cars. And then I took off at a run—down the bank, across the road, and into the trees on the other side of the highway.

It didn't take me ten minutes to reach the aunts' houses. I followed the stepping-stones to Lucille's front porch and knocked on the door. There was a window beside the door, and Aunt Lucille pulled back the lace curtain and peeked out at me. Her eyes widened, and I saw from the way her mouth flew open and how she threw her hand over her heart that I had caught her by surprise. She dropped the curtain and then the latch rattled and she opened the door.

"Junior. Is everything okay? Did something happen? To somebody?"

Funny how she didn't mention Granddaddy in particular. But she must've been asking about him. I shook my head. "I just have some questions. About my pop."

"Axel?" She waved me in and pointed toward the easy chair near the window. "What about Axel?" She reached around the back of her waist and untied the apron she was wearing. Then she slipped it off and carried it into the kitchen. Maybe my aunt figured she had to be all gussied up to see me, but I was used to women wearing aprons with flour and food spills on them.

Aunt Lucille's house was toasty warm. And no wonder—it had an oil heater sitting in the middle of the living room. That thing wouldn't cool down in the night like our woodstove did.

"Now," said Aunt Lucille, "what about Axel?"

All of a sudden I didn't know what to say. I stopped and started over a few times and finally I just blurted out, "Why did Granddaddy hate him?"

Lucille ducked her head a little and squinted as though I was some stranger come to her door, meddling in her family business. And in a way I was. But I was also her nephew, and with Pop gone, I figured if I wanted to know anything about his family I should hurry up and ask.

While she was making up her mind whether to answer my question we heard footsteps on her porch and then a knock at the door.

"My stars!" said Aunt Lucille. "That must be my sister." She went to the window and peeked out. "Just as I thought. Lillian is dying of curiosity. She hasn't talked to me in two months. And now, three minutes after you show up, that woman is on my porch with a tin of fudge. If she thinks she can sweet-talk her way in this door, she has another thought coming."

21

AUNTS
January 1942

Aunt Lucille's determination started to crumble the second her sister pushed the tin into her hand. She took a deep breath, and I could almost see the smell of fudge filling her up. She closed her eyes and breathed it in. Then she pulled herself together. "Lillian," she snapped. "What is *this* for?"

Aunt Lillian laughed, and her voice went sweet as chocolate. But it had a bitterness too, like Momma's cocoa powder. "Lucy, have a piece of fudge." She turned then and looked at me. "Why, Junior Bledsoe! Is that you? Do tell. Lucille, share some of my fudge with our nephew."

Lucille held the fudge out to me and I took a piece.

"Have another," said Aunt Lillian. She stepped inside and pushed the door shut behind her.

So there I was, with a piece of fudge in each hand, watching her and Aunt Lucille tiptoeing around each other. I tried to imagine them with Pop, playing together when they were all young'uns. But those two women

133

eyeing each other didn't seem like the kind of people who could have been small and childlike once upon a time. For one thing, they were both tall. And big-boned. Right now, Aunt Lucille's face was more serious than Miss Hinkle's in the middle of a handwriting session. Lillian was smiling, but I could tell she was all pretend—just trying to buy something with that fudge of hers.

Lillian sat herself down on the sofa. She patted the cushion beside her. "Sit, sister. And do taste the fudge. Tell me if I've lost my touch."

Lucille frowned and then kind of shuffled over to a straight-backed chair on the other side of the room. She set that fudge on a side table and turned her head away—like she was trying to forget it was there.

But the smell of that chocolate was strong. I couldn't wait a second longer. I popped one of the pieces into my mouth.

"How do you like it, Junior?" asked Lillian.

"Mm," I said. "Delicious." I licked the melting chocolate off my fingers.

"You're just saying that, aren't you? It's so good to see you. But why aren't you in school?"

Lucille glared at Lillian, then at me—like she was warning me not to talk to her sister. But why shouldn't I? I wanted to know some things, and I wasn't convinced that Lucille would answer my questions.

"I was asking Granddaddy about Woodrow Wilson," I said. "He started talking about the war and was real angry about something—he said it was Axel's fault. But then he just quit talking."

Lillian's eyebrows went up, like she was surprised. Then down, as if she was thinking. I had a feeling she knew something. She glanced at Lucille but didn't say a word.

We sat there quiet for a minute and then I said, "I got to thinking, maybe y'all would remember something."

"Well," said Lillian. Then she stopped.

"Yeah?" I said.

"Daddy never fought in the war. And he blamed Axel for that."

"Why?"

"Axel was having a hard time sitting still in school," said Lillian. "He couldn't think unless he was fiddling with something. Daddy would stand over him while he was doing homework, rushing him and saying how he didn't have all night to do one arithmetic problem. That made things worse. So finally Axel just up and quit. He could be mule-headed that way."

That sounded like Pop, all right. But what did it have to do with Woodrow Wilson?

Since Lillian was talking, I guessed Lucille wasn't going to be outdone. She grabbed up a piece of fudge and took a bite. Then she started talking. "Daddy took him to the mill and made him sweep floors. There was plenty of work there to keep him busy."

"And hundreds of machines," interrupted Lillian. "It

turned out, while Daddy thought he was sweeping up, Axel was studying the machines. And how they worked. By the time Daddy figured out what was going on, Axel was already helping to fix those machines."

"But he wasn't earning any money for it," said Lucille. "Daddy was all fired up about that—the boss man getting free labor out of his son."

"Your granddaddy didn't mind his son sweeping floors for no money," said Lillian. "After all, that was *his* idea, but fixing the boss's machines? That was another story altogether. But the boss refused to pay for Axel's labor. Said the law wouldn't allow him to hire a boy that young."

"The whole time, war was threatening," said Lucille. "And your granddaddy's draft number came up. Boy howdy—was he happy about that! He was all set to go and then he had the accident."

"Oh. His hand?"

"His fingers got caught in the carding machine and he lost half his hand before they could turn it off," said Lillian.

"Axel was the last person to work on that machine," said Lucille. "Daddy said he did it on purpose."

"Ridiculous!" Lillian declared. "Carding is dangerous that way. The machine has metal teeth to comb the cotton and separate it into fibers. If you don't watch yourself, it'll eat your fingers. Daddy must've been careless. On top of that, he didn't go to the doctor. Wouldn't let Mother come close to it with soap and water. So it started turning black."

Lucille nodded. "Gangrene."

"Finally one day our neighbor brought him some whiskey and while Daddy was passed out drunk he had a doctor tend to that hand. But it was too late. He couldn't save it."

"Thing was, Axel was the last person to work on the machine."

"You already told him that."

"The boy was only eleven years old. But Daddy said it was *Axel's* fault he couldn't play on the mill's baseball team anymore. And you know what made Daddy maddest of all?"

"What?" I asked.

"The war." They both said it together.

"He couldn't go off and fight," said Lucille.

"Oh, but he tried," Lillian added. "He was determined that nothing would keep him out of that war. He'd go outside every single day and practice shooting with his left hand."

"But the neighbors complained about the racket. So the police came and took his gun away."

"Daddy was sure mad about that. Mad enough to start a war all by himself. And I guess you know who his enemy was."

All of a sudden I felt sick to my stomach, thinking about my pop on the receiving end of Granddaddy's wrath when he was just a young'un. Eleven years old.

Lillian stood and shoved that tin of fudge into Lucille's hand. "Eat some more," she said. "It'll make you feel better." Then she offered some to me too.

I took one for each hand. "I reckon I better be going," I said. "But thanks for the fudge and for telling me about Pop."

After that cozy living room, the cold air hit me in the face. But I let out a big sigh of relief to be away from those two aunts, and when I did, I could almost see that sigh hanging like a frosty cloud in front of me.

I spent the day walking around Brookford. The town was a couple of hills with little white houses lined up along them. They reminded me of train cars that had come unhooked from each other. I walked up Red Hill, where Granddaddy used to live before we moved him in with us. Somebody else lived in that house now. But I stood in the street and imagined Pop inside at the kitchen table trying to do arithmetic with Granddaddy standing over top of him.

No wonder he left school.

There were other buildings in Brookford—stores, a gas station, a pool hall, and a couple of churches. The red-brick cotton mill where all those people worked was big enough to set half the houses right inside it. I figured Pop knew that place inside and out, considering he'd swept its floors and fixed the machines.

Somewhere down there on the river was a swinging

bridge. Once, when I was six, Pop took me to see it. I still remembered how scared I felt up so high and how the bridge rocked with every step we took. But Pop held my hand real tight and told me to hang on to the cable with the other hand. "Don't look down," he said. "Keep your eye on where you're going and you'll make it across just fine."

Someday, maybe I'd go looking for that bridge, but for now I wanted to get back to the school and sneak onto the empty bus that parked there during the day. I knew I could stay low until it was filling up with noisy young'uns. By then the driver wouldn't even notice me.

My plan worked. Even Ann Fay didn't ask questions, so I figured she hadn't missed me at school. In fact, playing hooky was so easy I had half a notion to try it again.

I never thought I'd be the kind of person who would do such a thing. But now, I felt like I could even *quit* school if I wanted to. Maybe there was a law saying I had to go. But nobody seemed to care enough to enforce it. My old pal Calvin Settlemyre was proof of that.

22

OXYMORON
January 1942

"I assume you were sick yesterday?" asked Miss Hinkle.

"I've got a lot on me right now," I said.

She peered over her glasses at me and started to speak. Then stopped. Then started again. "Yes, Junior. I know you do," she said. "But now you *also* have to catch up on the work you missed."

She'd taught a lesson on metaphors and similes, it turned out. And today she was teaching oxymorons. She wrote *oxymoron* on the blackboard and drew a line under it. Then she wrote *two contradictory words or ideas used together*. Under that definition she wrote *awfully pretty*. "That is an oxymoron," she said, "because *awful* and *pretty* contradict each other. It's essential, when writing or speaking, to always choose the right word."

She asked us to each think of an oxymoron, to write it on the blackboard, and to use it in a sentence.

It didn't take Janie Aderholt two seconds to think of one. She raised her hand and went to the board and wrote *pretty ugly*. Then she turned to Miss Hinkle and said, "The war is getting pretty ugly."

Next thing I knew, there was a list of oxymorons on the blackboard. *Sad smile, small crowd, only choice, loud whisper, sweet sorrow.*

The only thing I could think of that contradicted itself was *holy terror*, which I didn't figure she would count since I'd be stealing it from Granddaddy when he used it on Christmas Day. The other idea that came to my mind was *neighborly teacher*. And I sure wasn't going to write that on the board.

"Junior Bledsoe?"

Good grief! Did she have to call on me? I headed toward the blackboard, but I didn't have any idea what to write. I picked up the chalk and felt the grit of it between my fingers. Then it hit me that I had a perfectly good oxymoron. *Good grief*, I wrote. Only problem was I couldn't think of a sentence. I turned to the class and said, "Good grief!" And that's all I could think of.

"Excellent!" said Miss Hinkle.

Really? That was excellent? I couldn't believe it!

I saw Dudley's hand go up. Miss Hinkle gave him a nod. "Yes, Dudley?"

"He didn't come up with a sentence."

"Actually, *good grief* is often used by itself, as a sentence. Now it's your turn, Dudley."

I have to say I enjoyed watching Dudley's face go

from a smirk to a scowl. He dragged himself out of that chair and slouched his way to the blackboard. He stood there a long time and finally he wrote *cat fish*. Then he turned and faced the class. "The catfish meowed."

The whole class busted up laughing when he said that, and even Miss Hinkle couldn't help but crack a smile. Much as I hate to admit it, I laughed too. Dudley tried to smirk at me on the way back to his seat, but mostly he just grinned and strutted like a fighting rooster.

Marilyn Overcash went to the board and wrote *worst enemy*. Then she turned around and said, "If someone is your worst enemy doesn't that mean he's your best friend?"

"Very thought-provoking," said Miss Hinkle.

Worst enemy. Best friend. That didn't make any sense. By now, I figured I should be used to things not making sense. But I wasn't. I was as confused as ever.

23

FIGHT
February 1942

By February there was no denying that the war was cranking up. The newspaper announced that sugar would probably be rationed in the next few months. And maybe gasoline. On top of that, they were fixing to change the draft age.

I heard it first on Granddaddy's radio. Men from age twenty to forty-five would have to register. "What'd I tell you?" said Granddaddy. "Mr. Leroy is gonna be called up." To hear Granddaddy gloat about it, you'd think Leroy didn't have a wife and children at home who might worry about him.

It was a few more days until Ann Fay borrowed the newspaper from the Hinkle sisters and read it for herself. Then she brought it to school and I read the article on the bus.

"It doesn't look so bad," I told her after I read it. "Because he has more than three dependents. Yeah, he has to register, but they're not expecting men with three dependents to serve. Not right now, anyway."

"Not right now," said Ann Fay. "But that means later. Eventually they'll be calling him up too."

"Maybe it won't come to that. We're going to win this war. Soon."

A week later, the whole country went on War Time, which meant we had to turn our clocks ahead one hour. It was supposed to help save on gas. Granddaddy was downright hostile about anybody messing with the sun. "Franklin Roosevelt might think he's God," he said. "But he can't decide when the sun comes up, and he ain't making me change my clock."

To prove his point, Granddaddy got out of bed at the usual time—according to his watch—and when Momma brought him meals, he'd let them sit for an hour before he ate them. They were cold and he complained, but Momma didn't heat them up for him.

Of course his radio programs came on according to War Time, but since he mostly stayed in the bedroom and listened, it didn't much matter what time it was. The radio was full of news about our boys fighting the Japanese in some place called Bataan. And Granddaddy had lots of opinions on the topic. Never mind that he hadn't even fought in a war. He still thought he knew more about it than General Douglas MacArthur, who was leading America's battle against Japan.

"I've half a notion to sign up," Granddaddy said one morning.

He thought he could go off to some place in the Pacific Ocean? For the last three days he'd barely left the bed.

"That's gonna be hard," I said, "if you stay in bed all day."

He must've taken that for a challenge on account of he sat straight up and grabbed his shirt off the nail in the wall. He wiggled his legs over the side of the bed and started to put the shirt on, but he couldn't find the sleeve.

"Help me out, boy!"

I took the shirt from him and held it so his arms could go through the sleeves, and then I turned to go. "Button me up!" Like he was an army sergeant and I was a common soldier.

"I guess you're practicing up for war."

"Huh?"

"Giving orders, I mean."

"Hmph. Children, obey your grandparents. Look it up in the Bible."

I knew that wasn't in the Good Book. Not the grandparent part. But I kept my mouth shut.

"You should sign up. It's your patriotic duty."

I buttoned the last button and he pointed to his pants, so I took them off the other nail. "I'm not old enough," I said.

He nodded toward the portrait of his father. "Don't tell me you're not old enough. If Gideon Bledsoe could do it, you can too. Lie about your age. Big strapping boy like you could sneak in and they'd never know the difference."

"Okay, Granddaddy." I didn't mean *okay*—like I would do it. Just *okay*—like I'd say anything to shut him up and get myself out of the room.

By the time I could dress and shave and empty his chamber pot, I had to run to catch the bus. Momma shoved an apple-butter biscuit into my hand and sent me out the door. "I'll do the milking for you," she said.

At school I was still in a sour mood. And bumping into Rob Walker at the water fountain did not help matters one bit. I noticed a big red welt on his arm. And I guess I stared at it a little too hard because, all of a sudden, I felt someone twisting my jacket sleeve.

"What're you staring at?" It was Dudley's voice coming through clenched teeth. I turned and his face was right there—so close I could tell he ate raw onions for breakfast.

"Nothing," I said. "I'm not staring."

"Yes, you are. You're looking at my brother's arm. It ain't none of your business what happened to it."

"I wasn't going to ask. But now I reckon you gave yourself away. You did that to him, didn't you, Catfish?"

"You ain't talking about me and my little brother like that. Hear me, Bledsoe?" And before I could even see it coming, Dudley slammed his fist into my ear.

I stumbled backwards, but I wasn't about to take that sitting down. I steadied myself, balled up both fists, and went at him. Face. Neck. Stomach. For every time he punched me, I made sure I socked him back. I heard voices cheering for Dudley. And some hollered for me. One was louder than all the rest—Ann Fay screaming, "Stop it, Junior Bledsoe. Stop it. Here comes the principal."

Strong hands pulled us apart, and there was Mr. Hollar glaring at me and then at Dudley and back at me again.

"What do you boys think you're doing?" He half pushed us from the water fountain to his office. When we were inside, he shut the door. Hard.

My ear hurt. My jaw hurt. Some other places did too. "He started it," I said.

"Did not!"

"Did too. You hit me first."

"Hush," said Mr. Hollar. "I don't *care* who started it. *I'm* going to finish it. I should expel you for this kind of behavior. Bend over. Put your hands on your knees and keep them there." He reached for the big wooden paddle that hung off the front of his desk so that anyone could see it the minute they walked through the door.

He hit Dudley first. Dudley grunted. I snuck a peek at him. He squeezed his eyes shut and waited for the next hit. But evidently Mr. Hollar was watching me.

"Mind your own business, Junior. Eyes on the floor."

So I stared at the wooden boards and waited while Dudley took five licks. I heard five loud grunts. Being expelled wouldn't be so bad, I thought. If only Momma didn't have to know about it. At least, if Mr. Hollar kicked me out of school, I wouldn't have to decide to quit.

Then it was my turn.

It hurt like fire. But every time I took a lick I thought about Pop. If this was him back when he was a boy, Granddaddy would give him twice as many when he got home.

24

SURPRISE
February 1942

One morning about two weeks after I played hooky, I decided to slip off again. This time I wanted to find that swinging bridge. I wanted to stand on the bridge and remember. Remember me being scared and Pop helping me across.

Only thing was, I wasn't far into the woods when I heard some twigs snapping behind me. I stopped and listened. But all I could hear was the sound of a horse and wagon clattering down the hill into Brookford.

I started walking again, quiet as I could. And every so often I'd hear a noise and think I wasn't alone in the woods. But then I decided it was my imagination, so I stopped paying it any mind and kept going until I found the bridge. It was just a few rows of boards fastened to cables that stretched across the river. And there was a cable on each side for hanging on to and a pitiful row of slats to keep a body from falling off.

That bridge swayed with every step I took, and the water rushing below gave me the heebie-jeebies. It felt as if the whole bridge was moving upstream. My legs wobbled and I gripped the cable, hanging on to Pop's words. *Keep your eye on the other side.* For some reason, that put me in mind of Miss Hinkle and that confounded handwriting advice: *Keep thinking. Keep moving. Keep gliding.*

When I was halfway across, I saw a stranger come onto the far side of the bridge. I didn't feel like talking to strangers, so I turned and headed back to where I came from. That's when I realized who had been in the woods with me.

Dudley Walker.

And now Dudley was on the bridge, too. There I was, up in the air on a swinging bridge—trapped between two people I didn't feel like talking to.

Dudley came straight toward me. Fast. Like he thought he could scare me by making the bridge sway. Or maybe he wanted to knock me off. I hung on to the cables at the sides and did my own share of swaying— just to let him know I wasn't afraid. We got that bridge rocking worse than Granddaddy's chair when he was fired up about something.

Behind me, I heard the stranger yelling. "Whoa there. Whoa. Yee-owl."

Dudley was just about six feet from me now.

"What are you doing here?" I yelled.

"Following you, I reckon. Someone has to keep an eye on you."

"What I do is none of your business!"

"What if I make it my business? What if Old Lady Hinkle wants to know why her little neighbor boy wasn't at school? Somebody has to tell her the truth, don't they?"

I didn't figure Dudley would be running to tell Miss Hinkle about me coming to Brookford when I was supposed to be in school. But it was hard to tell. He probably wouldn't mind getting himself in trouble as long as he could drag me along.

The bridge was starting to settle down a little. "What do you want, anyway?"

He shrugged. "To be shed of that school. And that teacher. Probably the same things you want." He jerked his head toward the other end of the bridge. "Who's that?"

I'd almost forgotten about the stranger behind me. I turned and there he was. A tall man. He looked familiar. But why? He was hanging on to the sides of the bridge and trying not to drop his fishing pole at the same time. "Steady now. Steady boys." Then he looked right at me and said, "Axel? Is that you? I heard you was dead."

He thought I was Pop!

"Axel Bledsoe has passed on," I said. "Who are you?"

"Otis," the man said. "Hickey."

Otis Hickey. Of course. Now I remembered. Pop would buy car parts from him. And one time, when he needed a radiator, he even took me to the junkyard behind Otis's house. "Axel was my pop," I told Otis.

He nodded. He looked a little sad and faraway too, with his eyes just staring down into the water. "Me and Axel used to fish in this river," he said. "Axel was older, but he let me follow him around. Mostly to wherever Jerm Foster was working on a car. Axel liked getting grease on his hands."

Jerm Foster. Pop used to take me to his garage sometimes. I'd wander around, stepping over tools, and sniffing at the smell of oil and tires while I listened to the two of them go on about everything from mufflers to ignition switches.

Hearing Otis talk about the two of them gave me a warm feeling inside. I just sort of forgot about Dudley standing there listening. But after a while I noticed he'd sat down with his legs hanging over the side of the bridge. Come to think of it, sitting wasn't such a bad idea. So I did the same and Otis joined us.

There we were, just sort of floating above the river—a grand place to be on a school day, up at the height of the trees, with the river below us, washing on downstream. It soon turned and went out into the country.

Otis told me stuff Pop had never even mentioned. How Pop wanted to play baseball on the Brookford Mills team, only Granddaddy wouldn't let him. And how one day Pop walked out of Brookford with only the clothes on his back. "He'd had enough of this town and his people," said Otis. "Enough of his daddy, anyway. Hammer Bledsoe is a hard man."

"Yup," I said. "He sure is."

"I heard he went to live with Axel. I am kindly surprised."

"It was my momma's idea. Since nobody else wanted him."

Otis shook his head. "Hammer was a bad sort of fellow, some days—setting his children one against the other until they didn't know who to trust and who to hate. People say he grew up rough and passed it right on down the line."

When he said that, I pictured Gideon Bledsoe in his Confederate uniform, holding that gun across his chest. Granddaddy said Gideon was hard as nails. But I couldn't imagine it—an earnest-looking boy with kind eyes like that, turning as mean as Granddaddy.

Every now and again, someone would come across the bridge and stop to talk to Otis. Before I knew it, the noon whistle was going off at the mill and Otis was getting to his feet. "Time to shove in the clutch," he said. "Momma's expecting some fish for supper tonight." And just like that, he up and left.

But Dudley Walker was still there. He opened his lunch bag and pulled out a biscuit. "It was my daddy," he said.

"Huh?"

"My daddy put that welt on Rob's arm. Buckle end of the belt."

"Oh."

"He *could* pick on me, but he don't. Not that much, anyhow. Mostly it's just Rob. I try to lie and take Rob's punishment for him, but Daddy beats him anyhow. I don't know why he hates Rob so bad."

I thought about Granddaddy hating my pop on account of that accident and how that meant he couldn't go to war. And about Pop pulling away from me the day I turned eleven, which was the same age Pop was when Granddaddy lost his hand. It didn't make any sense, really. But still, the more stories I heard, the more I thought I understood.

"There's usually a reason," I said. "Even if it doesn't make sense to anybody else."

25

CAUGHT
February 1942

We snuck up to the school just before the last bell rang. I circled around below the back side of the building and came from the lunchroom end of things.

When I got on the bus, Ann Fay was already there. I walked right past her and found a seat near the back. Even before I sat down, I could tell she was on my trail. "Where you been, Junior?" She sat down beside me.

"Minding my own business. What about you?"

"I didn't see you today."

"I reckon you had a good day then, didn't you?"

She frowned. "I like seeing you. At least when you're not being mean. Are you feeling mean?"

Was I feeling mean? I shrugged. It was hard to explain what I felt, and if I knew what it was, I probably wouldn't be telling it to her.

"I heard you played hooky."

I didn't like the sound of *that*. "Who you been talking to?"

"Rob Walker said his brother seen you leaving school one day. He figured you'd do it again. And you weren't in class today."

"When did you turn friendly with the likes of Rob Walker? He's trouble and you ought to stay away from him."

"Rob didn't say it to me. Other people are talking too."

"Other people don't know what they're talking about."

"I don't think I believe you, Junior."

I shrugged. "If you don't like what I have to say, go sit with Peggy Sue."

Ann Fay hugged her books to her chest. "I think I'll do just that." Then she stood and headed for the front of the bus.

"And don't be spreading lies about me neither," I called after her. But I saw her whispering in Peggy Sue's ear the minute she sat down.

The next morning I tried to think of a good reason to stay home. I figured I was in deep dooky with Miss Hinkle and probably Mr. Hollar too. But when I told Momma I didn't feel good, she put her hand on my forehead and said, "You don't have a fever."

Miss Hinkle didn't say a word about me being absent from school. She called the roll same as every morning and made us practice our handwriting like usual, too.

The drill sentences on the board were:

Young man, grasp your opportunity.
Time and tide wait for no man.
Quibbling and quarreling are bad habits.

The way me and Dudley had been quarreling this year, I was sure it never crossed Miss Hinkle's mind that we had spent yesterday hanging around in the same place together.

Dudley ignored me until time for lunch. And then he plopped himself down at the table next to mine. "We ought to join the army," he said. "It'd make more sense than what we're doing here." All of a sudden it was like Dudley Walker had decided to be my pal.

If someone had suggested such a thing a week ago I would have said they belonged in the loony bin. But after hearing Dudley talk about his little brother getting beat up by his daddy, I didn't feel so alone anymore. Maybe we did want the same things in life. Like Miss Hinkle and that handwriting book said, *Union of interests brings union of minds.*

Now here Dudley was, talking about enlisting. Defending the freedom of America's children. That sounded good. Joining the army would earn me some respect, for sure. My picture would be in the paper. Granddaddy might even hang it on the bedroom wall.

But still, I wasn't planning to enlist. "You're crazy," I said. "We're underage."

"Lots of people lie about their age," he said. "And the army is desperate for soldiers. It's the patriotic thing to do."

I shook my head.

"Young man," said Dudley, "grasp your opportunity."

"You sound like some old lady schoolteacher."

"Watch your mouth, Bledsoe!"

When it was time for physical education, Miss Hinkle told me and Dudley to stay behind while the others went to the gymnasium. "I've been told that the two of you rode your buses to school yesterday. Is that correct?"

I saw the toe of Dudley's shoe making a figure eight on the wooden floor.

"Look at me. Both of you." I jerked my head up and looked Miss Hinkle in the eye. It was like staring at two bright shiny nails. Metal. Cold. "Were you on the school bus yesterday?"

"Yes, ma'am."

"Dudley?"

"Yes, ma'am."

"And where were you after that?"

I shrugged, waiting for Dudley to explain. But he let me do the talking.

"Don't shrug your shoulders at me, Junior."

"We went to Brookford."

"So you were truant?" That was her fancy way of saying I was playing hooky. "I will, of course, need to talk to your parents."

I couldn't let her do that. But how could I stop her? I started talking. Fast. "My mother has been real upset," I said. "On account of Pop dying. It would be best if you don't say anything. I'll do better, Miss Hinkle. I promise. I won't play hooky again."

Maybe Miss Hinkle did have a little bit of neighborliness left in her, because what she said next surprised me. "I'll give you one more chance. But if this happens again, I will be contacting Bessie."

26

AIM
march 1942

I wasn't about to give Miss Hinkle a reason for talking to Momma about my truancy. So I worked harder than ever. But the sight of my handwriting always sent Miss Hinkle fishing for her fountain pen and bottle of red ink. She kept returning papers marked up with criticism. *You can do better.* Or, *Sloppy. Do this over.*

One good thing about school—besides the time I dropped my pencil and Janie picked it up and handed it back to me—was that Dudley and I weren't constantly bickering. He'd bring his sack lunch and plop down at the table with me. Sometimes he'd tell stories on his daddy—about him whipping up on his brother or being happy drunk and making a fool of himself.

"We just need to leave out of here," he kept saying. "I heard on the radio where three thousand men from Catawba County enlisted last month. Now it's our turn."

"Those three thousand men were between the ages of twenty and forty-five," I said.

"So we'll tell them we're eighteen. The army ain't being that picky."

The worse I did in school and the more I listened to Dudley saying "Young man, grasp your opportunity," the more he made me believe we could do it. Some days when Granddaddy was dozing in his chair or poking around in Momma's business, I'd pick up that picture of Gideon Bledsoe and stare at it.

His eyes would hold me and I'd want to have a conversation with him. I sure would love to hear him tell me what it felt like to go off to war so young. And how did it feel to come home a hero?

One day Miss Hinkle assigned us to write essays on things we could do to help win the war from home. I wrote that I had already dug around in my shed for rubber and metal to take to the scrapyard. I would plant a bigger garden next year so food from grocery stores could go to the army.

I knew I should be buying war bonds, which was a way of loaning money to the government until after the war. Every copy of the *Hickory Daily Record* advertised them for sale, and every citizen was supposed to be buying them. But what if some citizens had to struggle to pay the light bill?

Maybe the best thing I could do was get a job. Then I could buy war bonds. And if I worked for a sock factory like the one Peggy Sue's daddy owned, I could even make socks for soldiers. But when would I have time for that? Between school and working around the house, I was doing good to catch the bus every morning.

In the essay, I mentioned that I could quit school and find a job.

That was the wrong thing to say in a paper for Miss Hinkle. The day after I turned it in, she called me into the hall. I didn't have any idea what I was in trouble for until I saw that paper in her hand. She flapped it in the air to show me that she disagreed with what I wrote. "Junior," she said, "I certainly hope you are not serious about dropping out of school. That will not benefit you or the war."

It was bad enough that she had to go and argue with my ideas. But on top of that, she started in on my handwriting. "I do not emphasize this for my own benefit," she said. "The Palmer method is designed to help you make a good impression when the time comes to pursue work. I want you, Axel Junior, to meet with success when you go out into the world."

Miss Hinkle just had to throw in Pop's name—to remind me *he* hadn't made such a good impression. To shame me into doing better than he did. She handed me a small book. It was *The Village Blacksmith*, by Henry Wadsworth Longfellow. "I want you to copy this poem in your best handwriting. And memorize it, too. Then you will have its message in your heart for the rest of your life."

"Yes, ma'am."

That poem was all about a hard-working, upstanding man who didn't owe any debt. I had no trouble reading between the lines, and I knew Miss Hinkle was trying to tell me to be different from Pop.

I copied the poem as best I could, in between all my other chores. But I didn't even try to memorize it. If Miss Hinkle thought she had talked me into staying in school, she was sure wrong about that. Instead, I turned in the poem and told Dudley I was ready to enlist.

"Atta boy!" Dudley thumped me on the back.

The next morning we walked right into the building like every other day—in case Miss Hinkle or Mr. Hollar or anyone else was watching out the windows. But just when I was ready to pass the auditorium doors, Mr. Hollar stepped out into the hall. He cast his eyes around like he was always doing, looking this way and that, but he was busy talking to a teacher and I didn't think he even noticed I was there. They turned and walked up the hall in front of me and went into a classroom.

Now all I had to do was make it past my room. Miss Hinkle was at the blackboard, writing a sentence in her perfect Palmer longhand. Seeing *that* made me want to run, but I tried my level best to look normal. I went out the back door and slipped past the building, sticking close to the wall so no one inside would see me from the windows. At the corner I started ducking from one tree to the next. Then I got antsy and took off at a run.

We had to go through Brookford to reach the recruiter's office. Dudley had said to meet at a certain hickory tree just before the swinging bridge. There was a hollow log there for hiding our schoolbooks. He was sitting on the log and smoking a cigarette—calm as pond water.

I leaned my forehead against a tree and closed my eyes while I tried to catch my breath. The rough bark of the tree felt good under my hands. I peeled some off and crumbled it in my fist.

"Want a smoke? It'll settle your nerves."

I shook my head. "Naw. I'm not nervous."

"Liar. I see you shaking in your shoes."

I didn't see how he could tell and I sure wasn't about to admit it. I turned and leaned with my back to the tree, sliding until my behind was sitting in the leaves. "I don't smoke."

He shrugged. "Look, there's nothing to be nervous about. Throw your shoulders back and march into that office like a soldier." Dudley stood and started across the swinging bridge.

"Ha! You look like a drunken sailor, is what you look like."

Dudley started singing, slurring his voice. "*Shipmates, stand together. Don't give up the ship. Fair or stormy weather, we won't give up, we won't give up the ship.*"

I just sat there staring. And laughing. Dudley Walker could actually be fun sometimes. I thought about the first time I saw him on that bridge and what he said he wanted—to be free of school and Miss Hinkle. To get out and see the world. He sat there listening to Otis tell stories on my pop. And then he started telling his own stories. About Wayne Walker.

He was right about what he said that day. We both wanted the same things. Not just to leave school behind us but to be shed of some other things, too. For instance, the way people looked at us on account of our fathers. We both wanted to earn our own respect in this world.

Dudley was on the other side of the bridge now. I hoisted myself up and followed him, keeping my eye on the other side so I wouldn't lose my nerve. I intended to go through with this.

So, when I was across the bridge, I took off at a trot toward the highway. We passed the cotton mill, marching and holding our heads up proud and puffing out our chests. We told each other what we planned to say to the recruiting officer—that our country needed us because we were young and strong and of sound mind. We wanted to protect the freedom of the world. I decided I would say what Franklin Roosevelt said—that it would be a privilege to fight for the future of America's children. The Germans and Japs and Italians were gangsters trying to take over the world, but we were too tough for that. I'd tell them I had a crackerjack aim and I intended to use it.

It was a long walk, but we finally made it there.

27

MISFIRE
March 1942

After all that walking, it felt good to just sit on a hard bench and wait. Dudley smoked one cigarette and then another. "Where do you get them?" I asked.

He laughed. "My old man. And his friends. Have to sneak them one at a time. My father is a happy drunk. He's fine with missing a few cigarettes when he's drinking. But I can't take too many too fast or he'll notice when he sobers up."

We sat in that waiting room for more than an hour. And I noticed that people who came in after us were called back before we were. Maybe their lottery numbers had come up. Maybe that explained it.

But we waited forty-five more minutes, and I was fixing to be mad. "God bless America! Where are they?" I asked. "We come here to help win the war and they leave us sitting like a couple of dogs by the side of the road."

I went outside and stared at the brick wall of the

166

building across the street. Being in town was like being stuck in my room with Granddaddy. Everywhere I looked, I saw walls when I wanted some trees. I needed the smell of pine needles and rotting stumps. The clean fresh air of the woods. I needed the feel of my gun in my hands and a squirrel or even a deer in my sights. I half closed my eyes and imagined the woods behind our barn.

"What you doin'?"

The trees in my mind disappeared, and now I was staring at that brick wall again. The smell of cigarettes pushed away the leafy, woodsy smells. Dudley was standing there poking me with his elbow. "You look like you're pulling at a trigger. Like you just can't wait to find yourself in this war." He laughed and slapped me on the back. "That's good. The recruiter is going to take to you like a turkey buzzard on dead possum."

"Dead possum? Dadgummit, Catfish. Is that the best you could come up with?"

Dudley laughed so hard he nearly choked on his cigarette smoke. And that got me to laughing, too.

"Junior Bledsoe!" That was the recruiting officer standing at the door. "Thought you wanted to talk to us."

"Yes, sir." I turned. "See ya later," I said to Dudley.

"Oh, no. I'm coming too."

The officer held up his hand. "One at a time."

Dudley spoke up. "Sir, we came together. We plan to stay that way."

We did? I didn't remember discussing this. But maybe Dudley was scared too. Maybe he needed me to make him feel brave. "If you don't mind, sir," I said.

The officer frowned. He stood there tapping his foot for a minute. "Follow me." He took us to a small office with no windows—just a desk with a chair and a short bench on the front side of it. "Sit."

I couldn't help but feel how close Dudley was on that bench. But it felt good. Like it wasn't just me facing the officer and his questions. If I didn't have the right answers, then more than likely Dudley would.

The officer left us there and we waited some more. "This is what it's like in the army," whispered Dudley. "They tell you to hurry up, and then they make you wait."

The desk had a metal lamp on it with a green glass shade and a pull chain. The lamp was off and the bare bulb in the ceiling didn't light the place up so well, but I could see a world map on the wall—marked with all the places the Germans, Italians, and Japanese were causing trouble.

Finally I heard footsteps coming down the hall. When the door opened, the officer had another man with him. He explained, "Two of you, two of us." As if this was some kind of contest we were in. As if he needed help to win.

I wished they had two chairs on that side of the desk, but they didn't, so the second officer just stood there with his arms folded across his chest. "What brings you here today?"

"The war," said Dudley.

The officer looked at me. "Yes, sir," I said. "The war." I pointed to the map on the wall. "The gangsters are trying to take over the world. We're not gonna let 'em."

"We?" asked the officer. He stared into my eyes and I knew he wanted me to explain.

"Me and my pal." It sounded strange to call Dudley *my pal*. But sitting there shoulder to shoulder, it seemed right, too. "President Roosevelt said we're all in this together. We aim to win this war, and it will take every last one of us."

"How old are you?" asked the second officer.

I hesitated just a second. I knew I wasn't a good liar. Dudley spoke up. "Eighteen, sir. Both of us."

The officer narrowed his eyes at Dudley. Then he looked at me.

I nodded.

The officer came around the desk, and what he did next surprised me. He put his hand on my face and rubbed at my chin with his thumb. I jerked my head away. He laughed. "Maybe you're growing a couple of whiskers there. Maybe not." He stepped in front of me and reached for Dudley. "What about you, pretty boy?" He turned to the other officer. "Can you give me a light here?"

At first it sounded like he was asking to light a

cigarette, but then I realized that no, he was mocking Dudley. Asking the other officer to pull the chain on the desk lamp and turn it in Dudley's direction. So he could search for facial hair.

Well, Dudley was kind of blond, and I reckon that made a difference. The officer rubbed on his chin. "I don't believe this one is eighteen," he said. I could feel Dudley tensing up beside me. He scraped his shoe against the floor, making that figure eight again, and making little growly sounds in his throat. The officer smacked him a little on the side of the head and went back around the desk. "They're just a couple of cubs. Momma bears won't like them leaving home."

"Tell me," said the other one. He looked at Dudley. "What do you have that this army needs?"

I heard Dudley swallow real hard. And I could feel the bench shaking. Maybe it wasn't him shaking it. Maybe it was me. But his foot was going like crazy against the floor. I watched it until I could almost see the number eight laying there sideways on the boards.

Finally he spoke up. "Sir, I'm a fighter. Just ask him." He jabbed me with his elbow. "I know how to go after the enemy. Put me in this army and I will track the enemy down and make him wish he was at the bottom of the sea."

I almost laughed when Dudley said that. I don't know why. Maybe it was nervousness. Then I realized it was my turn to speak. I had to convince them I was qualified to serve in the United States Army. "I've been hunting all my life, sir. My aim is dead-on perfect. I can shoot a turkey from forty yards. You know Sergeant York, sir? I'm that good." Of course it was stupid for me to say such a thing. But in that moment I was grabbing at whatever came into my head, and that's what showed up. After all, Alvin York learned to shoot the same way I did. It wasn't the army that taught him. He learned from living in the backwoods of Tennessee. "My pop taught me," I said.

The officer nodded. He picked his cigar out of the ashtray on his desk and blew a few puffs our way. He didn't say anything. The other officer didn't either. They both just sat there staring at us. Nodding.

What did that nodding mean?

Dudley lit up a cigarette. Everybody was smoking except me. And for some reason, all of a sudden, I had to have me a cigarette too. Maybe that would prove something about my age. I bumped Dudley's arm with my elbow. "How about a smoke?"

He squinted, and I knew what he was thinking. He was remembering how I told him I didn't smoke.

"I was lying," I whispered.

Dudley put the cigarette in his mouth and dug into his pocket. The one he brought out was bent, like all his cigarettes. Dudley leaned toward the desk and tapped the ashes of his cigarette into the ashtray there. He held the tips of those two cigarettes together until mine caught the light. Finally he handed it to me.

I put it in my mouth, and the sharp taste of tobacco set me back for a second. I let it sit there until I got used to it. I thought about eating lima beans—I didn't like them either when I first tasted them. That was years ago. But now I loved limas. I could learn to like tobacco too. I inhaled.

Oh, boy. I should have just let it sit there. Because holding a cigarette between your teeth is not the same as sucking in the smoke of it. It took me back to the first time I fired Pop's shotgun. I'd braced myself for the recoil like he said—but still, the kick knocked me backwards.

At least Pop was there to catch me and set me up straight again. Now, there was no Pop, only Dudley, making worried sounds in his throat. I yanked the cigarette out of my mouth and told myself to just suck it up and look smooth. But I didn't have control now. It was like the smoke was a giant hand squeezing my throat shut. I sat there coughing and pounding myself on my chest. Trying to catch some fresh air, but there wasn't any such thing in that little room.

Above all the commotion I heard the officers laughing. And Dudley was slapping me on the back. "What happened?" he was saying. "You smoke all the time and all of a sudden you start choking? Are you sick?" I knew

172

he was trying to convince the officers that I knew how to smoke a cigarette.

But they weren't believing him. Even I could see *that* through the cloud between us. They waited. Arms folded across their chests. They looked at each other, and I reckon they had some kind of secret signal because they both shook their heads. Then the one who brought us in there spoke up.

"Smoking don't make you a man," he said, and he looked at Dudley when he said it. "I'll give you thirteen or fourteen years. Not eighteen. Not old enough to go clear around the world without your momma's apron strings to hang on to."

He looked at me. "And you with the perfect aim. Just be careful what you point at. Because what if you hit it and it's not what you thought it was?"

28

CONSEQUENCES
March 1942

Dudley didn't say a word after we left the recruiting office. He marched out ahead of me, and I followed his trail of cigarette smells. I told myself I didn't *care* if he was mad. What was he to me?

Finally, after we were back in Brookford and had crossed the swinging bridge and were pulling our books out of the hollow log, he decided to talk to me. "Bledsoe," he said, "I never should've taken up with the likes of you. You're a moron, is what you are."

"Huh. If I'm a moron, then I guess that makes you an oxymoron."

He snorted. "You don't even know what that means."

"It means you're a bigger moron than I am. That's what it means." I did feel bad about messing everything up with that stupid cigarette, but I didn't let on. "They weren't going to take us anyway," I said.

"They would have. If you hadn't tried to act all manly when you obviously aren't."

"Oh, yeah? At least I can grow a beard if I take a notion."

That shut him up. At least for a little while. "Our goose is cooked," he said. "We played hooky and we can't even tell Old Lady Hinkle we joined the army. What're you planning to say?"

I shrugged. "I'll think of something."

We would barely make it in time to catch our buses and the younger grades would soon be pouring out of the building. Just ahead of us was the road bank that sloped up to the schoolyard and the area under the trees where Mr. Hollar and the teachers parked their cars. We waited for a car to go by and then we ran across the road.

Dudley dashed to the trees, but I waited so the two of us wouldn't be seen together. He moved from one tree to the next and then swaggered out into the open, holding his books with one arm so they bumped against his hip when he walked to the buses. He threw his head back, and I could tell he was whistling. Trying to act like it was every other day.

He rounded the corner of the school near the buses. I decided to go the long way. On the back side of the building was a set of steps going down into the furnace room. Wouldn't you know, the janitor was coming up with his mop bucket. "Bledsoe," he said.

I stopped. "Yeah."

"Mr. Hollar is looking for you. He said if I see you to

tell you to go on to his office and wait."

"Uh. Okay." I was almost at the back entrance of the school. I could go in, march up the hall, and make a few turns to Mr. Hollar's office. Or I could keep going. Take my chances at getting on the bus and riding away before Mr. Hollar figured it out.

I decided to take my chances. My bus was at the back of the lineup, and I was almost there. I picked up my pace—practically running—and hopped onto the bus, quick as I could, after some younger boys climbed on.

Mr. Hollar was in the front seat. Waiting for me. It was too late to turn and run. No matter what I did next, I was in trouble. So I just stood there, hanging on to the metal pole, and waited.

"Did you have a good day, Junior?"

I stayed quiet. What was I going to say?

"I asked you a question." Mr. Hollar's eyebrows pulled together, making deep lines that ran up into his forehead.

"No."

"No what?"

"No, sir. I did not have a good day."

"Off the bus, Junior."

Oh, boy. Looked like me and Dudley would be riding home with Mr. Hollar this time. I turned, and at the bottom of the steps, fixing to climb on, was Ann Fay. She threw her hand over her mouth when she saw me with the principal.

176

I glared at her and she kind of whimpered like a hurt puppy. She wouldn't have to ask if I felt mean today. I couldn't hide it if I tried.

Mr. Hollar stepped out in front of me and stalked into the school. I followed him up the wide concrete steps, staring at my feet and trying not to notice the students coming out at the same time. But I knew right when Janie Aderholt was beside me because I recognized her blue skirt and the penny loafers going past me down the steps.

"Hey, Junior," she said. "Where were you?" But I didn't answer or even turn to look because I had to keep following Mr. Hollar. And anyway, what would I say?

The principal's office was just inside the front school door.

Mr. Hollar pointed to a heavy wooden chair. I sat and waited. In just a few minutes Miss Hinkle came, sour as a pickle, through the door, and right behind her was Dudley. He didn't look at me, though.

Mr. Hollar demanded an explanation. I figured honesty was the best policy. "Sir," I said, "we volunteered for the army. Uncle Sam needs us."

"You did what?" He sounded surprised. Maybe he was even impressed. "How did that go?"

I shrugged. "Not so good, I guess."

He picked up that paddle on his desk and tapped it against his palm, making steady smacking sounds.

I could almost feel my backside stinging. I wished he would just get it over with.

"I should whup you both, but I suppose I'll let your parents figure out what kind of punishment you deserve." He handed us each a folded paper. "Bring these back signed by a parent. And since you like walking so much, you can find your own way home today."

That's how we ended up walking again—this time with cars and school buses blowing exhaust in our faces. Miss Hinkle drove past. She'd make it home a good half hour before I did.

I was bone tired and real grumpy. And worrying about upsetting Momma.

"My old man would beat me black and blue if he saw this note," said Dudley. "I'll tell my mother I missed the bus, and later, when Daddy ain't looking, she'll sign that paper for me. He won't know the difference."

Him saying that put me in mind of Momma standing between Pop and the rest of the world—making excuses for his behavior like she was protecting him from what people would say and think. But at least Momma never had to protect me from Pop. He just didn't have it in him to beat his family; I was sure of that. Probably because of Granddaddy whupping him. And besides, I did my level best not to cause Pop or Momma a minute of worrying.

But those days were over. Now Momma was always fretting over me. I didn't know what to do about that. After all, with him gone I had a mess of things troubling me too. And school was right there at the top of the list.

I wanted to go home and tell Momma I was accepted into the United States Army. That I'd be fighting for the freedom of the whole world. I couldn't do that. Not yet, anyway.

But one thing I could do was find a job. Now seemed as good a time as any to quit school. "I'm not even showing this note to my mother," I told Dudley. "Pop wanted me to drop out of school. I'm finally gonna do it."

Now all I had to do was convince Momma.

QUITTING
march 1942

Momma was at her ironing board by the kitchen table, sprinkling my blue plaid shirt with water from a Cheerwine bottle. She didn't even look up when I let the back door shut behind me.

"I'm home."

She spread the shirt over the ironing board and pressed the hot iron onto it. Steam rose around her like a cloud of anger. "Miss Pauline was here. You skipped school? What's gotten into you, Junior?"

I shrugged. I didn't exactly know how to explain. It wasn't like I was trying to be bad. Maybe Momma didn't deserve what I was putting her through, but I didn't ask for the hand I was dealt, either. And I had had enough. "I can't do it," I said.

"Exactly what can't you do?"

"High school. It's useless. Why does my longhand have to look like the Palmer method? And that nonsense Miss Hinkle talks about, poetry and grammar and figures of speech—what does any of that have to do with getting along in the world? Do you even know what a participle is, Momma? Much less a dangling one."

"Axel Bledsoe, Junior!" Momma set her iron down hard. "Don't you dare take that tone with me."

I took that to mean she didn't have any idea what I was talking about. But she wasn't going to admit it, either. "See?" I said. "You're doing just fine in life without knowing certain things. And Pop could tear a car to pieces and throw it all in a heap. He wouldn't know a participle if it was on top of the pile. But he could put it all back together."

Momma almost smiled.

"The reason I played hooky was, I tried to enlist."

Well, that set her back. "Junior!" Worry covered over her face like wrinkles on that shirt.

"I wanted to do you proud, Momma. Get some honor for the Bledsoe name. Lord knows we could use it. I could fight for freedom with the best of them."

She stood, stiff as starched laundry, with the iron pressing into my best shirt, not even noticing the scorched smell it was making.

"Momma! The shirt." I grabbed at the iron, but it was too late. The blue plaid had a brown triangle pressed into it. When Momma saw that, she let out a shriek. "For crying out loud!" She took off across the kitchen with her face in her hands, ran into her bedroom, and slammed the door.

I stared at that scorched shirt. She'd just made it for

me a few weeks ago. And I knew we didn't have money to buy more material.

"Now look what you done." That was Granddaddy, standing not three feet away, nosing into my business. "Better unplug that thing before you burn the house down."

I reached up to where the cord of the iron connected to the light socket and pulled the plug. And I set the hot iron over on the cook stove, where it couldn't do any damage. There was a pot of potatoes and peas with bits of ham stewing there. "You might want to dish up your own supper," I told Granddaddy. "I'm going to tend to the animals."

I went to the barn and milked Eleanor. "I should quit—right, Eleanor?" I didn't know why I was asking her. I just couldn't see me going back. As far as I could tell, the only good thing about school would be sitting behind Janie. I knew she didn't like me. Maybe she liked me a little more than she liked Dudley, but that wasn't saying much. And besides, by now she'd probably heard about the two of us playing hooky. She wouldn't be impressed with the likes of me.

When I was finished tending the animals, I strained the milk and took it inside. Momma had supper dished up and we sat down to eat but she wasn't starting any conversations.

"I'm sorry, Momma," I said. "I'll pay for the shirt. I'm

not going back to school. With the war on, this country needs workers. I'll take a job at Brookford Mills, making cloth for uniforms. It'll be my bit for the war. And I can buy war bonds and pay the bills. Maybe we can even get ahead."

Momma squinted. "Axel hated that place. And you're just like him. You'd hate it too."

"Maybe. Or maybe I'll like bringing home some money. Doing something more in this world than he did." I shouldn't have said that. I wasn't trying to put him down or hurt her feelings or anything. It was just a fact. I tried to soften it then. "Maybe I just want to be where he was," I said. "See the machines he fixed. Heck, I'd even sweep the floors."

"Junior, I want you to go to school."

"I know you do, Momma. But I can't."

"Yes, you can. And you will." Momma shook her fork and little bits of broth came flying at me. I saw her lip quivering like a leaf in the wind. I took a bite of biscuit and she kept on preaching. "If you keep this attitude, Axel Bledsoe, Junior, you're likely to turn out just like your father."

"I know," I said. "Acorn don't fall far from the tree. Least that's what I hear."

I was trying to sound tough—like I didn't care if she compared me to Pop. But much as she loved him, I knew she didn't mean it as a compliment. Sure, I could do some

183

of the things people admired about him. Fixing cars and helping perfect strangers. But lately I was real good at hurting her the way he could, too.

I finished my supper and then went to work cleaning her treadle sewing machine, which needed oiling. Maybe she'd see that if I didn't have homework to do I could actually help out more around the house.

Later, when I crawled into bed, Granddaddy wandered around the room. I watched his stockinged feet go past my head and thought about the things I'd heard from Aunt Lucille and Aunt Lillian.

"What's it like?" I asked. "At the mill. What kind of jobs do they have?"

Granddaddy's feet stopped in their tracks over by the bureau. "What business is it of yours?"

"I need a job," I said. "I'm not going back to school."

"Well, if you ain't Axel made over again."

"Yes, sir," I said. "I'm a big disappointment. What kind of jobs they got?"

"Sweeping floors."

"What else?"

"Operating machines. Packing. Shipping." Granddaddy walked past my head again, his feet sending up little clouds of dust. "I reckon you could sweep up. Like your daddy did."

"I thought he fixed machines. I could do that."

"Boy, you ain't laid eyes on one of them machines

and already you're wanting to fix 'em? Your daddy learnt that a little at a time."

Granddaddy reached for the string hanging down from the light in the ceiling and the room went dark. The bedsprings creaked when he climbed into bed. "You can't live here and work there. You gotta live in Brookford, where they can own you. Rent from them. Buy food on credit at the company store. Be in debt the rest of your life."

That was something I hadn't thought of. "Does everybody at the mill live in Brookford? I'm a hard worker. They should be proud to have the likes of me there."

"If you're so good, how come you ain't sticking it out at school?"

"That's different," I said. "School is a bunch of hot air, if you ask me."

Granddaddy laughed. "I'll tell you what," he said. "How about in the morning you wake up and listen to the radio and I'll go to school for you. I have a feeling me and that pretty schoolteacher will get along just fine. I could clean her blackboards and if I'm lucky she'll keep me after school and teach me to talk right. I could sing to her, even."

Then Granddaddy started singing. "*Let me call you sweetheart. I'm in love with you. Let me hear you whisper that you love me too.*" And when he did, he sounded a lot like Pop always did when he came in at night. His deep voice alone could make you forget all the headaches and worries he'd just put you through.

Granddaddy sang to the end of the song, then rolled over and thumped his pillow. It wasn't two minutes later that I heard him snoring.

"Sweet dreams," I muttered.

30

BROOKFORD
March 1942

"Okay," I mumbled when Momma called me in the morning. I almost crawled out of bed. But then I remembered. I wasn't going. I turned over and tried to go back to sleep, but in no time she came knocking again. This time I didn't answer.

"Junior! You're going to be late."

I pulled the pillow over my head. But that didn't stop me from hearing her open the door and walk into the room. "Hammer," she said. "It's time to kick this boy out of your room."

His room? That made me good and sore. Momma turned his radio all the way up and marched back into the kitchen, flapping her dishcloth at my head on her way out.

Between me being mad and the sound of the radio blaring, I knew I wasn't going back to sleep. So I crawled out of my bed and turned the radio off. Granddaddy had a few words to say about that, but I ignored him and got dressed.

A plate of cold grits and eggs was waiting for me at the kitchen table. I ate and Momma fidgeted around by the stove, keeping her back to me the whole time like a wide wall of anger.

"After I milk Eleanor I'm going to clean up and go looking for a job," I told her.

Momma pushed the cupboard door shut extra hard.

I intended to apply for work at the mill, and the sooner the better, so after my chores I climbed on Grover and headed for Brookford.

Grover was tickled to be on the road again and wanted to trot. Evidently he approved of me quitting school. It felt good to be out on the highway with the March wind nipping at my ears and the bright sun trying to warm them up. Right before Whitener's store I saw a gray car at the side of the road—a 1937 Chevrolet. A woman about Momma's age stood there staring at it, hugging herself and looking like she didn't know whether to kick that car or bust into tears.

I tugged on the reins and Grover pulled to the right. "Whoa." I waved to the lady and hopped down. "Got a problem?"

She stopped hugging herself and started talking with her hands going every which way. "The car just stopped." Her voice sounded like she was on the edge of tears. "I have to get it to Jerm Foster, somehow."

"Ma'am, your car sure is a beauty. I betcha I can fix it."

The woman frowned. More than likely she didn't believe me.

"I tell you what," I said. "I'm going right by Jerm's place on my way to Brookford Mills. If I can't fix you up, I'll stop in and send Jerm out to help. Unless you want to ride my mule with me."

She looked at Grover and wrinkled her nose.

I laughed. "Let me take a look. But first, are you sure you aren't out of gas?"

Now the lady looked downright disgusted with my mechanic skills. "Sometimes that happens," I told her. "My pop was a mechanic. You'd be surprised how many people think they have car trouble when all they need is gas."

I lifted the hood and first thing I did was pull the dipstick. I ran it between my thumb and forefinger to clean the stick. I didn't have a rag on me, so I wiped my fingers on the dry grass at the side of the road. Then I put the stick back into the engine and pulled it out again. "You've got oil," I said. "That's good. Never let it get too low or you'll have big problems on your hands." For some reason, when I said that, I heard Pop's voice, sounding all sure of himself. I sure hoped she could see that I knew what I was talking about.

I poked around the engine, and it didn't take long to find that a spark plug had come loose. "Aha! Here's the problem, ma'am. Once I put this spark plug back in you'll be hitting on all six cylinders." I tightened it as best

I could with only my fingers. "You might want to have Jerm take a spark plug socket to that," I told her. "Want me to start the engine for you?"

"No, no. I can do that."

I figured getting behind the wheel was too good to be true. But anyway, she started the car and it cranked right up, purring like a tomcat. The lady sat there shaking her head and smiling like I was a miracle dropped out of heaven.

I closed the hood, and by the time I walked back by her window, she had her hand stuck out to give me a shake. When she saw grease on my fingers she changed her mind, but she did stick a folded dollar bill between my fingers. "For your trouble," she said.

"No, ma'am. I can't take this. I didn't do anything, really. And besides, I enjoyed it. Honest, I did."

"Of course you can take it. Do you have any idea how much trouble you just saved me?"

I didn't, but I thought about Pop and how he would help people for free even though we had bills to pay. I sure needed to show Momma I could pull my weight around the house. So I took it. That dollar bill seemed like a sign that I would succeed. It proved that I could earn money and respect too.

Now I had a hankering to stop by Jerm Foster's garage. The man who was working on a car in there was skinny and had deep-set blue eyes just the way I remembered him. And he recognized me too. He smiled right off when he saw me. "I could pick you out of a crowd for Axel Bledsoe's boy," he said. Jerm started to offer me his hand but I guess he thought twice about it, because of the black grease on his fingers.

I stuck my hand out and it had grease, too. "I just fixed a loose spark plug. A lady wanted to pay you to do it, but then I came along."

He laughed and shook his finger at me. "I reckon you got it honest. Axel was always taking jobs out from under my nose. I wish I could say I taught him everything he knew. I did teach him a lot, but that boy had himself a knack."

I liked hearing Jerm talking about Pop that way, and I wanted to hear more. "I bumped into Otis Hickey," I said. "Over on the swinging bridge a few weeks ago. He said my pop was down here every chance. Did he work for you?"

"Once in a while. If you could call it that." Jerm laughed. "To Axel, fixing cars was all in a day's play. I had to bully him into taking money for it."

"That sounds like my pop, all right."

"How's your granddaddy?"

Ornery as a bulldog. That's what I wanted to say. But I didn't. "Same as always," I said. "He don't do much except holler a lot about war and how we ought to kill the Germans. And now there's the Japanese to be mad at. They killed Russell Crump at Pearl Harbor. Did you know Russell?"

Jerm nodded and his clear blue eyes clouded over. "I could tell you what that boy ate for breakfast. Biscuits with mustard and livermush. He was a good fella and his heart was in the right place when he enlisted. But he was too young to die." Jerm stopped, looked at me. "How old are *you*? Aren't you supposed to be in school?"

I shook my head. "Naw. I'm fixing to get me a job at the mill."

Jerm squinted at me, and I could tell from the look on his face that he wasn't going along with my idea. "You should be in school."

"I can read and write and do figures," I said. "And the things they make me sit through in that class don't have a thing to do with getting along in this world. My momma needs me to help make our way."

Jerm nodded. "Is that what she says?"

"I'm fixing to do her proud. Show her what kind of man I can be." I started backing toward the door. "I better shove in the clutch and step on the gas. Can't find a job sitting around like this."

I rode right by Aunt Lillian and Aunt Lucille's. They lived on that ledge between the road and the river. From there it was just a few minutes to the mill.

There was a small brick building to the side of it with a sign that said *Office*. After being in the bright sunshine it took my eyes a few minutes to adjust to seeing inside. "Can I help you?" asked a woman standing in front of a filing cabinet.

I took off my hat. "Yes, ma'am. I need work. With the war on, I figured production is picking up. I can work hard. And maybe you knew my pop. Axel Bledsoe."

She shook her head. "I'll tell the boss you're here." Just past her desk was a door. She opened it and stuck her head inside. "Mr. Hefner, do you know Axel Bledsoe?"

"He's dead," came a deep voice from inside that office.

"Oh." The woman turned red as a beet pickle then. "Uh, I mean. His son is here."

"I see." The man in the office coughed—a nervous cough—like he was embarrassed that I probably heard him say Pop was dead. "Send the boy in," he said. But then I heard his chair scraping the floor, and just when the lady motioned me in, he appeared at the door.

The man stuck out his hand. "Mark Hefner," he said. "And you're like a carbon copy of your daddy."

31

DRIVING
March 1942

Mr. Hefner pointed to a ladder-back chair, so I took it. He perched on the edge of his desk. "Axel was a genius with machines and I wanted him to work for me. But he didn't like this mill. Said he couldn't breathe in here."

"Pop liked country air," I said. "And farming and fixing cars. But *I'm* looking for work, sir. And he taught me all kinds of stuff. I fixed a car on the way over here today."

Mr. Hefner nodded. "Sounds like you're a chip off the old block." When he said that, I just knew he was going to hire me. But he started talking about Granddaddy. "I heard Hammer is staying at your house now."

"Yes, sir."

"Brookford isn't the same place without him."

I wasn't sure how to take that, since I knew if Granddaddy left us right now, our house wouldn't be the same either. But that would be a good thing. Maybe Mr. Hefner was thanking me for taking him out of there. "Well, he thinks Brookford is the cat's pajamas."

194

Mr. Hefner leaned forward. "Here's a little secret. Hammer didn't actually like Brookford when he was here. And Brookford didn't much like *him*. But still, he was part of the scenery, and a lot of rough fellows live here. A mill village isn't all bad, but it has its drawbacks. Your daddy did right to get out of this place before he started a family."

Was he saying my pop left because he didn't think Brookford was a fitting place to raise his young'un? I didn't ask the question, but Mr. Hefner seemed to be reading my mind.

"Axel didn't want this life for you." He leaned forward and tapped his pen on the desk. "I can't hire you, Junior. For one thing, if I have an opening, I'll hire someone from Brookford as a matter of principle."

So Granddaddy wasn't making that part up!

"But here's the most important reason. Axel Bledsoe wasn't cut out for life in a mill village. He headed out to the country because he was trying to do better by himself and those who came after. I suspect you'll do best to stay there, too."

Mr. Hefner stood, and I could tell that the discussion was finished. Evidently he thought I was just a country boy who couldn't make it even in a small town like Brookford. If I came there to get me some respect, I sure hadn't found it. He held the door for me and I walked past the secretary's desk and kept on going out into the chilly air and bright sunshine.

A horse and wagon clomped up the street, and a car pulled into Stewart Elrod's gas station across the way. Up the hill, on the porch of one of the little wooden houses, a woman opened the door and called for her young'un to come back inside.

It was all I could do not to go peek inside the mill. But I climbed on Grover and rode back out through Brookford. I didn't look to the left when I went by my aunts' houses, and I didn't slow down at Jerm Foster's garage either.

But I stopped in at Whitener's store in Mountain View. Otis Hickey was leaving with a big dill pickle in his hand as I was coming in the door. "Hey," he said. "I remember you. Axel's boy." Then he kept on going. "Gotta get a wiggle on. Momma is having a bad day with her arthritis."

I asked Miss Whitener if she could put me to work.

She shook her head. "I wish I could, Junior," she said. "But I've got my children to help me—after school hours." She looked hard at me, and I could see she was disapproving. "You didn't quit school, did you?"

"I reckon I'll be getting a wiggle on too," I said. And then I left real fast before she could ask any questions.

By the time I was home, Leroy's truck was sitting in our lane, but it appeared that he was inside talking to Momma. I figured she was crying on his shoulder about me quitting school. That meant I'd be hearing a lecture from him.

I put Grover in the barn and watered and fed him. When I headed to the house Leroy was sitting on the back steps, waiting for me.

"Your truck misbehaving?" I asked. "Need me to fix something?"

He shook his head. "She's running like a clock. Hop in." He stood and headed for the truck, then climbed in the driver's side and waited for me to climb in the other door. "Don't worry, Bessie'll hold supper for you. I told her I was taking you for a drive."

"Yes, sir." He was up to something. People didn't just take drives anymore. Not with the war on and everyone trying to save wear and tear on their tires. Not to mention using up gas. I didn't want to hear any sermon he might preach about me leaving school, but I couldn't figure how to escape it. "Where we headed?"

"You name it, Junior."

I wasn't expecting that, and what's more, I especially wasn't expecting my answer. "Hog Hill." I mean, it's not like I thought about it before he asked. But once the words were out of my mouth I knew I wanted to see the place where Pop died.

Leroy squinted. "You sure?"

I nodded. "Unless that takes too much gas?"

He shook his head. "Watch what I do," he said, and he cranked up the truck. He put it in reverse, eased out the clutch, and pressed on the gas. "You watching?"

"Yes, sir." I wanted to tell him I could do that with

my eyes shut, but I didn't. He drove to Hog Hill without saying a word about school. In fact, he didn't say much of anything. Just smoked his cigarette and explained why he was downshifting, how to let out on the clutch, and other stuff I could write a book about—if I was allowed to use my left hand to do it.

Wasn't long before we were at Hog Hill and headed down the holler toward Peewee Hudson's sweet potato house. It stood there all by its solitary self with no cars or farm wagons or anything around it. "I reckon nobody's buying sweet taters this time of year," I said. "Maybe I should've come on a Friday night when Wayne Walker and the rest of them boys would be here."

Leroy pulled into the grass beside the block building. "Maybe," he said. "What were you hoping to see?"

I shrugged. "I don't know. I'd like to know where they found him."

There was high grass growing in the side ditches on both sides of the road. And some bare wisteria vines hanging off some trees. I got out of the truck and walked around and tried to imagine. Was it here on this little mound? Did he stumble over that rock? Or was it over by that fence post?

There wasn't any way to tell, really. And no one there to ask. Everything was quiet as death. Only thing I heard was the sound of somebody's dog off in the distance, howling.

I turned and headed back to the truck. "Might as well go," I said.

Leroy climbed in the passenger side. "You fixing to drive us home?" he asked.

Well, I reckon my jaw dropped near to my knees when he said that. I stopped in my tracks. "Really?"

Leroy nodded.

He didn't have to ask twice. I ran around to the driver's side of the truck and climbed in. I sure didn't need him to tell me how to crank it up. I put it in gear and eased out the clutch just like I was supposed to, but the truck jerked when I did. "Easy," said Leroy. "Take your time and let up on the clutch the same as you push on the gas. You'll feel when it's right."

I did what he said. At least I think I did. But I still made the truck jerk. It reminded me of trying to smoke— it looked a whole lot easier than it was. The truck was on the road then, heading toward home, and I didn't have to concentrate so much on using the clutch.

"According to the law," I said, "I'm not old enough to drive or have a license."

"That's what I hear," said Leroy. "But I reckon nobody cares too much about that around here. Matter of fact, Homer Jarrett has been letting his son Ned drive to church on Sundays since the boy was nine. Far as I can tell, he hasn't been in any trouble over that."

"Pop always said I was too young."

"Aren't you the man of the house now?" asked Leroy. "And you've got more than your share of responsibilities. You've had them for a long time, I reckon."

I knew what he meant. That Pop wasn't always the man of the house like he should've been and I was used to picking up his jobs. Maybe Leroy even respected me for that. I just nodded.

"In my book that makes you old enough to drive. But that's just my opinion and it's probably not worth two cents."

I thought about all the times I'd begged Pop to let me drive and he wouldn't have anything to do with it. Now here was Leroy giving me a chance. "If you ask me," I said, "your opinion is worth a whole lot more than a couple of pennies."

32

FISHING
April 1942

I was in the garden walking behind the plow when I heard the dogs barking. I looked up, and there was Dudley standing at the edge of my garden. "Whoa!" I tightened Grover's reins.

Dudley pulled a cigarette out of his pocket and lit it up. Then he fished another out and offered it to me. "Have a smoke?" He laughed. "Or maybe you ain't been practicing."

"What you doing here?"

"Wanna go fishing?"

"Sorry. I'm trying to put food on the table for my momma and me."

"Catfish is food. And I know the best spot on the river for catching 'em. They don't call me Catfish for nothing. Look, I'll help you with whatever you're planting and then we'll go fishing."

I thought about that. Would he actually lift a hand to help me in the garden? I knew Momma would sure like some fish to fry up for supper. "All right, then," I said. "Grab that hoe and start making some rows."

We worked steady for an hour. I have to say, Dudley Walker could actually be useful when he put his mind to it. After we finished up, I poked my head in the back door and told Momma I was going to the river to catch us some catfish for supper.

"What about the peas you were going to plant?"

"They're in the ground, Momma. Dudley helped me."

"Dudley?"

"From school."

"I thought you quit school." Her voice was bitter.

"Dudley," I said, "come inside and meet my mother." He stepped just inside the door. "Momma, this is Dudley Walker."

I saw her eyes go narrow when she heard his last name. She probably knew, in an instant, that he belonged to Wayne Walker's family.

"He helped me work the garden," I reminded her. As if that would prove Dudley wasn't as bad as his old man.

Momma sighed. "Catfish sounds real good. I'll count on it, then."

We took off to the river and climbed down the bank by Jacob Fork Bridge. Then we waded upstream to the spot where Dudley said we'd catch some catfish sure as shooting.

There's something about sitting on a riverbank with

the smell of earth and moss and the feel of an April breeze in the air that makes you forget how you might not even like the person sitting beside you. More and more, I was thinking maybe Dudley wasn't so bad after all.

"How's school going?" I asked. "Reckon I will never play baseball now."

"Other than that, be glad you escaped," said Dudley. "How do you like being the man of the house?"

I shrugged. Him saying that reminded me of what Leroy had said the other night when he let me drive his truck. "I reckon I been the man of the house for a while," I told Dudley. "Seeing as how my pop had trouble living up to the title. It didn't start the day I left school or even when he died. I'll get by. You watch."

Just then Dudley's fishing pole gave a jerk. "Holy catfish," he said. "I hooked me a big one."

We didn't talk much after that, because all of a sudden fishing was real good. I caught two and he had three before we were interrupted.

If we'd been watching, we might have seen Wayne Walker coming down the trail toward us on the other side of the river. But we weren't paying attention and then there he was, hollering across. "Been looking for you, boy."

The muscle in Dudley's cheek twitched and his Adam's apple moved up and down, so I figured he was in trouble. "Yes, sir. Here I am."

"What you doing?"

"Catching us some supper, Daddy. We got five good-sized fish already."

Wayne grunted. I guessed that meant if he had a quarrel with Dudley, he might just let it slide.

I couldn't help but think about how I had a quarrel with Wayne. He wasn't somebody I bumped into very often, and I was glad of it. The last time I saw him, Pop was tuning up his car. But I decided this was my chance to ask some questions. "Sir," I said. "Remember me? I'm Axel Bledsoe, Junior. And I've been wanting to talk to you."

Wayne tilted his head. "Go on."

"That night when my pop died. Me and my momma never did find out what exactly happened. Did you and him fight or something? Did he get a bad batch of somebody's liquor?"

Wayne shook his head. "Sure wish I could help you, son, but I don't know any more than you do."

The way he called me *son*—it made the chills come over my arms. But I decided I was a man now, and I better not be backing down. "I'm guessing you gave him a ride over to Hog Hill? And maybe sold him some of your moonshine on the way?"

Wayne frowned. "That right there, son, is where you're wrong. I wasn't even at Hog Hill that night. Whatever happened to your daddy never made it to my ears."

I doubted that very seriously, but I decided not to

press the point. After all, I didn't want him being mean to Dudley on my account.

As it was, he made Dudley stop fishing and go to the house with him. "You been lollygagging around on the riverbank long enough, boy. Bring them fish of yourn and clean 'em up."

"Junior caught two of them."

"Don't look like he's going any place. If fishing's good as you say it is, he can catch more."

Dudley swore under his breath. "Sorry, pal," he said. "I'll make it up to you."

And to be honest, I believed he would, too. After all, hadn't he helped me work up the garden? Dudley hoisted himself to his feet while I pulled the string of fish out of the water and handed them over to him.

He followed his father up the path into the woods. It was a strange feeling, watching the two of them walk off together. Except they weren't together. Not side by side, anyway. Wayne tramped up the hill like he was fixing to miss his supper if he didn't keep a move on. And Dudley trudged after him, about fifteen feet back, as if he wanted to turn and come the other direction.

Dudley wanted to get away from his old man and I just wanted mine back.

33

PLAN
April 1942

After Sunday dinner I went to the rocking chair on the porch, fixing to catch myself a snooze, when along came Dudley. "Sorry about taking all the fish," he said.

I shrugged. "It's all right. I caught two after you left."

"I have a plan," he said.

"And what would that be?"

"You wanted to know about your pop, right? Like what happened to him that night?"

I stood when he said that. "Let's go," I said. After all, there was no reason for Momma to hear him. We walked around the back of the house to the big oak tree with Pop's block and tackle hanging from it.

I pointed to a sweet potato crate. "Sit." I took the other one. "Now," I said, "Momma won't hear what you were fixing to say. What was it?"

"I was saying, let's go to Hog Hill and see what we can see."

"I already did that. Leroy Honeycutt took me and there was nothing to see."

"And when was that? What time of day?"

"I don't remember what day. It was about five o'clock."

"Right. But Friday night—now that's a different story. And my daddy won't be there this weekend because he's going to Avery County, where his people are from. We could catch them fellers by surprise. Walk in there and demand some information."

I just stared at Dudley. "Why?"

"I thought you wanted to know."

"But why do you care?"

Dudley shrugged. "You want to go or not?"

I thought about that and figured yeah, I did want to go. So I said, "What time?"

"Late. After those men have been drinking and playing cards for a few hours they'll be more likely to talk."

"What if they're more likely to fight? When my pop was drunk you didn't really want to hear what he had to say. Momma'd just put him to bed and let him sleep it off."

Dudley shook his head. "We have to go late. If we don't, somebody'll see us."

"You talking about sneaking out?"

"Well, yeah. You wasn't fixing to ask your momma for permission, was you? I've got it all figured out. We'll borrow a car."

"Your daddy's? I thought he was going someplace."

"Of course not my old man's. What do you think I am? Stupid?"

"Well, whose then?"

"Who lives right up the road from you? And has a '35 Plymouth?"

"Miss Hinkle? You're out of your cotton-pickin' mind."

"Whaddaya say?"

"I say you're stupider than a dangling participle and an oxymoron put together. That's what I say. Miss Hinkle will never let us borrow her car."

"Of course not. But who's asking?"

I couldn't believe my ears. I mean—Dudley was suggesting we just up and steal Miss Hinkle's car? "Look," I said. "Sure I want to find out what happened to my pop, but what good's it gonna do me if I'm sitting in the jailhouse in Newton? I ain't stealing a car."

"Stealing?" Dudley shook his head. "I believe the word I used was *borrow*. Like Miss Hinkle says, it's important to choose just the right word so people will understand your meaning."

Well, I was catching on to Dudley's meaning and I knew that taking Miss Hinkle's car without asking was not borrowing.

"I bet she keeps the keys in it all the time. We'll meet behind her garage at eleven on Friday night. Old ladies like her and her sister will be sound asleep by then. Still, just to be on the safe side, we'll push the car out of the garage and onto the road before starting it up. We can run over to Hog Hill and be back in an hour."

"No," I said. "I won't do it." How did Dudley become my friend anyway? Was he a friend? I didn't know. But I did know one thing. I wasn't about to take Miss Pauline and Miss Dinah's car without asking their permission.

"You're scared," Dudley said, sneering at me.

"It's wrong, Dudley. I can't do it. I'll sneak out late and meet you just short of their driveway at eleven. But I'll have Grover and he'll be hitched up to the farm wagon."

Dudley groaned. "And get home at five in the morning? We might as well forget it. I guess you don't want to know what happened to your pop like I thought you did."

"Okay, then. I'll bring Grover and you can climb on his back with me. It'll be quicker if he's not pulling the wagon."

Dudley shook his head. "Just think about it," he said. "We won't be stealing it because we're bringing it back. After all that woman has put us through, don't you think she owes us a little something?"

"There's nothing to think about," I said. And I meant it, too.

But after he left, I couldn't stop thinking about it. What a confounded stupid idea! I thought about it when I was doing odd jobs at the sawmill and when I was planting cotton for a farmer near the crossroads. From there, Hog Hill was just a few more miles down the road. It was hard to put Dudley and his stupid idea out of my mind.

I spent the week doing a little bit of this and a little bit of that—for whoever I could talk into hiring me.

On Friday morning after I milked Eleanor, Momma told me to take two quarts up to the Hinkle sisters' house. Miss Pauline was at school and Miss Dinah was friendly as always. But that didn't stop her from fretting about my education. "Junior, who would've guessed that you would leave school before my sister did? Are you sure you made the right decision?"

Seemed like everybody was determined to put guilt on me.

I just shrugged. "So far, so good," I said. "I've been picking up work here and there. Helping Momma out."

Miss Dinah carried the milk into the kitchen. I stayed on her closed-in back porch with the ferns and wicker furniture. She had a table full of seedlings started— getting ready for gardening.

Then I saw something else. The spare car key on a hook by the back door.

I glanced into the kitchen. Miss Dinah was busy rinsing out the Mason jar, so, quick as a wink, I reached up and pulled that key off the hook.

"Want a molasses cookie?" she called.

"Uh—no, thank you, Miss Dinah." I slipped the key into the pocket of my overalls.

All of a sudden I felt hot all over. I knew I should put it back. But here came Miss Dinah with the jar all clean and dry. She handed me a quarter, and when I dropped it into my pocket, I heard the clink of the coin against the key.

"Thank you, Miss Dinah," I said. "We sure appreciate you buying milk from us."

"Your momma's lucky to have such a good son," she said. "You're a credit to her name."

I wished she hadn't said that. Because there I was, walking out with a stolen car key. To make matters worse, I caught sight of the sign they kept by the door. BACK DOOR FRIENDS ARE BEST.

I was a back-door friend. Or used to be, anyway. Right that minute I wasn't acting like any kind of friend at all. I should take that key and put it on the hook where it belonged, but Miss Dinah was standing there watching. I'd have to 'fess up and I couldn't do that. After all, she thought I was a good boy. A credit to my momma's name.

That's what I wanted to be. But I also wanted to go to Hog Hill.

34

HOG HILL
April 1942

Granddaddy was snoring in the middle of a Yankees game. So far this season, DiMaggio had a two-game hitting streak and that was the end of that. Yesterday he got no hits and this game wasn't looking any better. Either Granddaddy had already given up on him or he just couldn't stay awake.

I was worried sick about that key in my pocket. I sat up and pulled on my clothes and waited for the chiming mantel clock to tell me when it was ten-thirty.

Finally it was time, and I slipped out of the house. Of course Butch and Jesse had to crawl out from under the porch and try to tag along. "No," I said. "Stay home. And keep quiet, you hear me?"

It didn't take five minutes to walk up the road to the Hinkle sisters'. I could see Dudley's dark shape against the white garage building and his cigarette glowing in the dark.

"You lose your mule?"

"Don't get smart with me, Catfish."

212

"I looked in the car. She didn't leave the key in there. Not even under the seat."

That was my chance to back out. We could fetch Grover and head over to Hog Hill that way. But the truth was, I didn't want to ride a mule to Hog Hill. I wanted to drive Miss Hinkle's car. "I got the key."

"By golly, Bledsoe. I didn't think you had what it takes. Let's go."

So we opened the car doors and Dudley pulled the car out of gear. We pushed, one on each side, until we had it out of the garage. Then Dudley, who had made sure he was on the driver's side, reached in and steered it so that the car headed toward the road. "Hop in," he said. And he slid under the steering wheel.

"Look, I borrowed the key. I should be doing the driving."

"Nope, Bledsoe. I'm the one who thought of this. And anyway, how many times have you been behind a steering wheel?"

"Lots," I said. That was true—because when Pop fixed cars, I'd sit behind the wheel and dream. Dudley didn't need to know I'd only driven once in my life. But for all I knew he hadn't ever driven a car himself.

Evidently he *had*, because he got it moving just fine. Next thing I knew, we were on the highway and heading toward the crossroads.

"Your daddy let you drive?" I asked him.

"Yeah, only he don't know it."

"What does that mean?"

"I drive around sometimes when he's passed out drunk. He don't stop me, so I reckon that means he lets me. Right?"

"On the road?"

"Sometimes. If I take a notion."

Seemed like it took longer to get to Hog Hill with Dudley driving than it did when I went with Leroy. I kept looking over my shoulder for a cop car or somebody else to be trailing us, but this time of night there wasn't much traffic.

Dudley knew right where Peewee Hudson's place was. He drove the car down past the sweet potato house and turned at a wide space in the road. "Getting situated," he said. "In case we need to leave in a hurry." Then he drove back up the road and jolted to a stop in the weeds.

"Whoa!" I said. "You're gonna end up in the ditch! Or scratch up her car!"

Dudley switched the engine off. "You're just scared. Want a cigarette to calm you down?" He laughed and pulled one out of his pocket, but he waited until he was out of the car to light up.

The countryside was bright from a full moon. I could see horses and wagons and vehicles parked in the weeds. A couple of horses nickered back and forth and I wondered if they were here every Friday night. By now they'd probably become old friends with each other— like Pop and those men inside the potato house.

When we came to the door, we stopped. The voices inside were low and rumbly. Someone cussed real loud, and for a second there I thought maybe an argument would break out. Should we knock? Was this like a private club and we needed a password? Dudley, who had been so big and cotton-pickin' brave up until now, stepped back and motioned for me to go first. "You're the one looking for information," he said.

I decided to go in without knocking. But when I tried the doorknob, it wouldn't budge.

We heard some chairs shuffling and some scurrying around, and I knew right then that they were tucking their moonshine away. It took them a few more minutes to make everything look proper, but someone finally opened the door. I couldn't see the man's face very much because the light was behind him.

"I have some questions," I told him.

"Shoot."

"Listen," said Dudley. "This here is Axel Bledsoe's boy. He needs some answers about what happened to his pop. And you better not leave him out here in the dark."

The man just stood there for a long minute—probably to let us know he wasn't about to be bossed around by a couple of boys who weren't even old enough to serve in the army. But then maybe he decided we were old enough to raise a ruckus if we took a notion. Because he nodded and stepped back. The light from the room hit his face and I knew in an instant he was the deputy who told us about Pop dying. So Momma was right when she said the police was probably in on the drinking and gambling.

Dudley poked me in the back. "Get moving, Bledsoe."

I pushed the door open and walked into a room filled with smoke and the smell of cherry cigars. And whiskey breath.

It was the way Pop smelled when he stumbled into the house at night, singing *"Let me call you sweetheart."* It was the memory of me and Momma stripping off his coat and shoes and his britches, then tucking the covers around him so he could sleep it off. It was the sound of Momma's crying coming through the bedroom walls. It was a whole lot of worry and hoping, and trying not to give up.

I almost choked on the smells and the memories. Dudley pounded me on the back and threw his arm across my shoulder.

That smoky room went silent except for the shuffling of a few feet. And I heard someone's pocket watch ticking. I looked around the room. There were a couple of rough tables and cards and ashtrays. And men around those tables with fat cigars clamped between their teeth. Staring. Like everybody was waiting on me to say something.

"What happened?" I asked. "I know my pop died somewhere around here, but if anybody knows *why*, they're whispering it behind my momma's back. I'm ready for somebody to come out and say it. Was he drunk?

Did one of you get him riled up about something?"

Nobody said a word.

"Well, don't all of ya speak at once," said Dudley. "He won't be able to hear you thataway. Did somebody give him a bad batch of shine?"

"Ain't no moonshiners here," said a hefty-looking man in overalls.

"Yeah, on account of Wayne Walker being otherwise occupied tonight," said Dudley. He didn't explain about being Wayne Walker's son, but some of them knew that already. He went on talking. "What about that night? Was Walker here then?"

A whole bunch of them started shaking their heads no. It seemed real. I mean, I didn't see them looking around to see how the other ones were going to answer. They just shook their heads like it was the God's honest truth.

"What went on that night?" Dudley pushed the door shut and leaned against it. "Me and Junior ain't leaving until you tell us what you know."

It was quiet as a snowy night, at least for a minute. And then finally one fellow spoke up.

"Axel was here. He hitched a ride with somebody, but I don't know who. And he had a little money on him. So he was gambling—laid it all on the table. Said he had a good feeling about it. Said his wife would be proud of him for bringing home the bacon. But then he lost. And he started looking real sick. Like he couldn't believe he just turned that ten dollars into dust. He stopped playing then and sat there staring, until all of a sudden he stood up. 'I need some fresh air,' he said. He stepped out and didn't come back. Later one of the fellers stumbled onto him there by the light pole. By the time the rest of us got to him, he was gone."

"His heart gave out," said the deputy.

"That's what the coroner told me and Momma," I said to the deputy. "But how do I know you aren't covering up something? What you doing here anyway? Aren't you supposed to be the long arm of the law?"

The deputy nodded. "You guessed it. That's what I'm doing here. Making sure every little thing is aboveboard and legal as a court case." He stood there with his arms folded. Right behind him on the inside wall was a door.

"Well, then," I said, "how about you open that door? How about you show me just how legal every little thing is?" I crossed my arms too. And looked him in the eye and waited.

He snorted. Then he dropped his hand and pulled out his pocket watch. He glanced at it, then turned the face around for me and Dudley to see. "Boys, I do believe it's past your bedtime. He narrowed his eyes. "How'd you get here anyhow? I know you're too young to drive."

I could feel myself biting my tongue half off. Here I was talking to a policeman and fixing to leave in a stolen car. What if he wandered out past those other vehicles in the field and found the Hinkle sisters' Plymouth? But there were horses out there too, and they gave me the perfect answer. "Horse power," I said. "I've been riding mules since I was four years old."

He nodded. "How about you go climb on that mule and pretend like you never did see this place." He leaned in close so I couldn't help but smell whiskey breath. His voice was low and mean. "You forget you were ever here and I promise you I will too." And just to make his point, he pulled his star-shaped badge from his pocket. He wiggled it back and forth in front of my face. "Like I said, my job is to make sure everything that goes on around here is in accordance with the law."

It sounded like he was making some kind of deal with us. I could take him up on it or I could say we weren't leaving until he opened that door. But I knew he was threatening me with trouble if I pressed the point. I also knew it wouldn't do me any good. Even if he did open it, the only thing I'd see was empty sweet potato crates. I knew they had their moonshine tucked out of sight.

I turned to Dudley. "Some people think they're above the law," I said. "I don't want nothing to do with their kind. Let's go."

35

GUILTY
April 1942

When the door shut behind me and Dudley, I took a second or two to just stand there and breathe in the clean night air.

Dudley socked me on the shoulder. "Let's leave outta here," he said. "Your mule is waiting." Maybe he was trying to get a laugh out of me. More likely he was hoping the men inside were listening.

On the way back to the car I stopped by the light pole. Dudley kept walking, but I stood there wondering. Was Pop facedown? Did he go quick?

All of a sudden it didn't matter so much exactly how he had died that night. What mattered was that he was on Hog Hill, with the likes of those goons. I started talking to Pop—right out loud.

"If you had to die, did it have to be here? Do you realize what people think every time your name comes up? *He's the drunk that died over at Hog Hill.* I can just see them shaking their heads and saying what a pity it is. Feeling sorry for me and Momma. Well, Pop, I don't want people looking at me and thinking what a shame it is that I was born to the likes of Axel Bledsoe."

I stood there and listened for explanations or maybe an apology, even. But the only thing I heard was insects in the grass and somewhere off in the woods the sad sound of a hoot owl. I kicked the light pole. "You just had to leave us with no respect, didn't you, Pop? I sure hope you're happy."

And then Pop talked back to me. I mean, not really—I didn't hear his voice talking in my ear. But the sound of him singing so strong and powerful was filling my head. *Amazing grace . . . a wretch like me.* I felt myself starting to cry. But there was no way I was doing that—not with Dudley waiting in Miss Pauline's car. So I walked away from the light pole and leaned against the back of the car and tried to shut the sound of Pop's singing out of my mind. Except I didn't want to shut it out. I wanted to hear him singing. I wanted the sound of it to wash over me like river water on a hot day.

So I let that song roll across my mind in Pop's voice, one verse after the other. Then, right in the middle of *when we've been there ten thousand years*, I felt Dudley thumping me on the back. "Jump in the car," he said. "Quick. Someone is fixing to leave out of Peewee's."

Sure enough, I saw the headlights of some vehicle that was backing out. If they caught us with Miss Pauline's car I'd be the one bringing disgrace on Momma's head. I couldn't blame that on Pop. I bolted like a skittish cat and hopped into the car.

Dudley cranked the engine and let the clutch out, fast—too fast. The car jerked and then stalled. "Calm down, Dudley," I yelled.

"Shut up. I don't need you hollerin' at me." He cranked it again. This time he only jerked a little and got us out on the road and heading toward home.

I looked back over my shoulder and saw headlights turning out of Peewee's place. "He's coming this way."

"Shut up, Bledsoe. I can see that." Dudley stepped on the gas.

"Whatever you do, don't wreck this thing. What if it's the deputy following us?" I wanted so bad to know it wasn't the deputy. But I made myself look straight ahead. "See any red lights in your mirror?"

"If I do, I'll outrun him."

"No you won't!" I yelled. The road here was dirt and I could just see Dudley skidding into the side ditch.

Dudley cackled. "Calm down, Bledsoe."

That car followed us all the way to the cotton gin at the crossroads. When we stopped at the intersection it pulled up right behind us. Dudley was nervous. I could tell because he jerked Miss Pauline's car when he tried to take off.

Then the other car turned and headed east. But first, the driver gave his horn three short toots—like a warning.

I *knew* it was the deputy, reminding us that he was the one holding the star-shaped badge. And the power.

Still, at least he turned and went the other way. "Phew! That was close," said Dudley.

We only had a few miles to go, and I could not wait to be rid of that stolen car. "Hurry!" I said. Dudley pressed on the gas, and the car took off like a hound dog after a rabbit. "Whoa! Slow down. Thunderation, Dudley, if you wreck this, we'll be sleeping in the jailhouse for sure!"

"Make up your mind, Bledsoe." Dudley went speeding down the hill toward the river. I hung on to the door handle and prayed. *Lord, make him slow it down.* Finally he started braking. From the river it was only about a mile to home. As anxious as I was to get this over with, I did not tell him to hurry up.

Back at the Hinkle sisters', I half expected to see Miss Pauline standing in her empty garage waiting for us. Dudley turned the headlights off. Thank goodness for the full moon. As it was, I thought he was fixing to scrape the side of the building when he turned in. But we didn't, and Dudley handed me the key. "I reckon you know where this came from."

I had to be rid of it. The sooner, the better. So I snuck to the back door and listened for sounds inside. I saw that the door between the kitchen and the back porch was closed. I pulled the screen door open and hung the key on the hook, quick as I could.

But what if they'd already noticed it was missing and

suddenly it was hanging back up again? I changed my mind and flicked the key under the wicker chair sitting near the door. I bumped a fern on a plant stand and the sound of it wobbling practically scared the pinto beans out of me.

I steadied the plant, and just when I was shutting the door, I saw a light come on inside the house. "Heaven help!" I whispered. "I woke them up." I shut that door real quiet and then I took off running like a moonshiner with the law on his tail.

Dudley was waiting behind the Hinkle sisters' garage. He started running after me. "What's your hurry, Bledsoe?"

"I think they heard me."

"Those old ladies are never gonna catch you. *I* can't even keep up."

"They could call the police."

"You're imagining things. I'm sure the sisters don't go calling the police every time the house creaks. Hey, how about I sleep in your barn? I'm beat."

"And take my chances on Momma catching sight of you in the morning?"

"Don't worry. I'll leave before daylight. There's no telling what could happen if I'm not there when my family wakes up."

I decided to sleep in the barn too. That way I could run Dudley off at the crack of dawn. But first I grabbed the milking bucket off the back porch so I'd have an excuse for being out of the house when Momma woke up.

Dudley was asleep in a heartbeat, but I couldn't just fall off like that. My mind went back and forth between worry and guilt. My ears were tuned for the sound of that deputy's car coming up the lane. When I did sleep, I dreamed about red lights flashing and Pop singing and Dudley swearing. I woke up and Dudley was gone.

The sun was working up its courage to face the day, so I decided to get a head start myself. Eleanor was sleeping in her stall. "Rise and shine," I said, nudging her to her feet. She bawled the whole time. "Never you mind," I told her. "Ain't none of your beeswax what I'm doing here so early or where I was last night." I put some oats in her bucket and pulled up the milking stool. "You don't have any idea what it feels like to be Junior Bledsoe. So don't be judging me."

When I took the milk inside, I heard Momma stirring in her room. I poured the milk into jars and set them in the icebox. Momma came into the kitchen squinting. And yawning. "Have mercy! You did the milking already?"

"That boy stayed out all night," yelled Granddaddy from the bedroom.

Good grief! I couldn't get by with anything. "I slept in the barn," I told Momma. "Granddaddy snores too loud."

"Wasn't snoring when I heard you go out the back door."

"Okay, Granddaddy. But I still slept in the barn."

"Hmph. Bet you think I wasn't a boy once." Now he was leaning on the doorframe between his room and the kitchen. "I could teach you a thing or two about sowing some wild oats."

Momma was, for sure, awake now. She put her hand on my arm. "Is there something you should be telling me?"

"I slept in the barn," I said. "There's nothing more to say about that."

She leaned in and sniffed. "Why do I smell cherry cigars?"

And why didn't I think about me carrying that smell home? "Momma," I said, "if I walked into your room right now I'd smell cherry cigars. The scent of them never left when he did."

"Maybe." She pulled away. "Or maybe you've taken up smoking. Junior, we don't have money for foolishness. And that Walker boy. If he's anything like his daddy. I beg you to stay away from him."

"The way Calvin Settlemyre avoids me?" I asked. "Because, after all, I might be just like Pop. Momma, I've never touched a drop of liquor. I promise you."

"Acorn don't fall far from the tree," said Granddaddy. He was standing not two feet away from me and Momma. And it was like she believed him more than me.

"Your father promised too," she said. "But it didn't stop him from drinking."

I probably shouldn't have blamed her for thinking ill of me like that. After all, my name was Axel Bledsoe. "Well, if you don't believe me, then," I said, "I reckon you didn't call me Junior for nothing."

I heard her gasp, and the sound of it was ragged. I wasn't trying to hurt her. "Momma," I said, "you watch. I'm going to do better than Pop did."

So far I hadn't accomplished much in that department. In fact, I was failing. Sure, Pop was a drunk, and everybody knew it. But nobody could say he was a car thief.

36

NEWS
May 1942

I was in the garden, planting squash hills and minding my own business, when I heard Ann Fay's voice behind me. "Hey, Junior. Look who's in the paper. The real Sergeant York. He had to register for the army."

"I'll look in a minute," I said. I pulled a few seeds out of the paper poke and dropped them into the ground.

She parked herself beside me, right in the dirt. "The president registered too. Only he won't have to serve on account of having polio."

"No," I said. "President Roosevelt doesn't have to fight because he's already serving our country—meeting with world leaders and making important decisions. And the reason he signed up was every man between forty-five and sixty-five has to get a draft number. He just turned sixty."

"I know that," said Ann Fay. "Back in January. I saw it in the paper."

"It's all propaganda, you know. Same with Sergeant

York. People see pictures of them signing up and it makes them want to register too."

Ann Fay turned real quiet then and put the paper on the ground so she could cuddle Jesse and Butch. "I want me a dog," she said. "That way, if Daddy has to go off to war, I'll have somebody else to love me while he's gone."

"Dogs are a dime a dozen," I said. "Pop got Butch from Garland Abernethy, and I found Jesse in the side ditch."

Ann Fay snorted. "Huh, I ride up the road practically every day and never once have I seen a dog in the ditch waiting for me to take it home." She kissed Butch and then Jesse on the tops of their heads. She scratched them behind the ears and stared into space like she forgot I was even there. I went back to hoeing and after a while I heard her again.

"What if they pick Daddy's number? And what if he don't come home?"

I probably should have been more understanding. After all, if Leroy was called up, I'd be scared for him too. Still, I couldn't help thinking Ann Fay should be glad she even *had* a daddy to worry about. "Don't be fretting about something that hasn't happened yet," I told her. "Speaking of worrying, your momma's gonna think the bus forgot to drop you off."

"School let out early today," she said. "On account of sugar rationing. The teachers have to do the registrations. Did Bessie sign up?"

"Not yet. But she will. All the baking she does, we're gonna need sugar."

"Yeah," said Ann Fay. And then she finally told me her real reason for dropping by—besides bringing me the paper, that is. "Rob Walker said his brother Dudley stayed out all night on Friday. Wonder who he done that with."

Ann Fay had my attention for sure. But I just grunted, not letting on that I knew what she was talking about.

"Some people are just trouble, is what they are."

"Yep," I said. "Like Rob Walker." I covered the seeds with dirt. "Why're you talking to him anyway?"

"He was telling somebody else. I just happened to hear it. He said Dudley was with you."

I didn't like where this conversation was heading, and I especially didn't like thinking about what would happen if certain people found out where I was on Friday night. But I told myself to stay calm.

"You covering something up, Junior?"

"Yup. And they're called squash seeds. Wanna help?"

"Can't. I got my school clothes on."

I looked at her and shook my head. "And there you are—sitting in the dirt. What's your momma gonna say?"

"My dress is just fine," she said. "But where'd you go on Friday night?"

"To bed. Actually, I slept in the barn. Granddaddy snores."

"Rob said Dudley came sneaking in the house with hay in his hair. When his daddy found out, he took a beating for it."

I started hacking at a thistle coming up through the dirt, hoping she didn't see worry on my face. "Wayne Walker sure ain't like Leroy Honeycutt," I said. "Count your blessings on having Leroy for a daddy, Ann Fay."

She stood up and brushed the dirt off the back of her dress. "Reckon I better go. Like you said, Momma'll be fretting. Don't worry, Junior. I won't tell my daddy what people are saying about you and Dudley."

"That's big of you," I said.

Ann Fay stood there scowling like she was expecting a thank-you for being so neighborly and all. Maybe she *was* doing me a favor.

"Thanks for the report. And the newspaper."

Evidently that's what she wanted to hear, on account of she turned and walked off. I sure hoped her momma could get the red dirt out of her skirt tail.

But I will say, she had me worrying. And wondering about Dudley. Did he know all along he would take a beating for what he did? Why would he take that chance just on account of me and my pop?

I couldn't stop wondering about that. If Dudley was in trouble, would I be next? How did I know Ann Fay wouldn't go telling Leroy what she heard?

37

DOFFING
May 1941

Two days later, Leroy came by the house. I couldn't tell if he'd heard anything suspicious sounding about me or not. But at least he didn't preach any sermons or ask me what I'd been up to. "How's the job hunt coming along?" he asked.

I shrugged. "I do odd jobs here and there. But it's hit or miss. I need something I can count on, like a factory job."

"And how is that better than going to school?"

I shrugged. There wasn't a good answer for his question, so I just said, "School used to be okay. But this year it was useless."

Leroy nodded. "Maybe everything feels useless right now. It might take a while, Junior."

I didn't ask him what he meant. I was pretty sure he was talking about me getting over Pop dying.

"I'll tell you what. How about I ask Mark Hefner to give you a chance over at Brookford?"

"Really?"

Leroy nodded. "Really."

The very next day, Leroy came by after work and told Momma that Mr. Hefner had decided to give me a chance. "I'll drop Junior off at the mill," he said. "And pick him up on my way home."

I couldn't believe it was that easy. The next morning we passed all kinds of people walking through Brookford, heading to the mill with their lunchboxes. I felt right proud to be joining them.

I went into the office building and it was like Mr. Hefner was waiting for me. "Junior, I'm glad you're here." He offered his hand.

"Thank you, sir. I'm glad too. I'll even sweep floors if you need me to."

Mr. Hefner shook his head. "I have a real job for you. Doffing. At the end of the day, drop by my office and we'll talk about your future here. Let's go on over to the mill."

"Yes, sir." I could hardly believe it. Not long ago he'd said he couldn't give me a job. Now he was talking about my future. And all because Leroy had put in a word for me.

Mr. Hefner led the way to the factory building. "You'll be on Louise Canipe's spinning frame. You'll take off the filled spools and put empty ones on. The frames do most of the work automatically and Louise keeps it all running smoothly. She won't like it if you start daydreaming or get behind. That cuts down on her production."

"Yes, sir," I said. "But I won't be daydreaming."

I noticed right off that it was hotter *inside* the mill than out. Noisier, too. Before Mr. Hefner opened the next door, I heard machinery clacking away. He took me into a huge room with high ceilings and tall windows. First thing I noticed, besides the racket, was how it looked like it was raining inside that room. But what I was actually seeing was cotton dust floating in the air.

Machines—or frames, as Mr. Hefner called them— filled that huge room from one end to the other, looking like they each had a thousand spools of white thread spinning away. Belts ran up toward the ceiling and across the room. Lots of people scurried here and there pulling levers, tying threads, moving spools, and I don't know what-all.

Louise was wearing a canvas apron. She pulled out a tool that looked like a nut pick and was digging around in the frame with it, cleaning out lint, I think. But lint was everywhere, so what was the use of that?

She looked me over while Mr. Hefner practically shouted to her that I'd be learning to doff. I thought Louise could at least say hello to me, but she just gave me a nod, thanked Mr. Hefner, and went back to work. Something told me she didn't like having a beginner working on her frame. Or maybe she just didn't feel like shouting.

A few feet away there was someone else, a fellow who looked old enough to be serving in the war, snatching spools of thread off the frames and dropping them into a metal cart. Mr. Hefner led me over to him. "Watch," he said.

The man reached into another cart and picked up empty spools.

Mr. Hefner let out a high-pitched *woo* sound to get his attention. "Jake, this is Junior," he yelled. "Train him."

Jake nodded. "Yes, Mr. Hefner." I doubt the boss even heard him because he was already heading back to some peace and quiet. Jake stuck out his hand. "Howdy," he yelled. "Here's how it works. See these spools?"

How could I miss all that spinning white stuff? It was making me plumb dizzy.

Jake picked up a handful of empty spools, dropped them on some posts, and quick as could be, he fastened thread to each one. When they were all done the frame started up again and the spools turned white with thread wrapping around them.

He pointed to a section of spools that had stopped. "Help me."

I tried to snatch the spools off fast like he did, but when I dropped them into the metal cart I knocked his spools over. And he wouldn't let me straighten up the mess.

"That's it," shouted Jake. "Take these two sections." He pointed from where we were standing all the way to the end of the row. "I'll do the rest. For now. Later, I'll give you more." And off he went.

I took a deep breath and wiped at the sweat running

down my face. By this time I was staring at another section of empty spools. It didn't take me long to start thinking about fixing cars.

And wouldn't you know, Louise frowned and made a hurry-up motion with her hands. It was looking to be a long day. I almost started praying the spinning frame would break down. Maybe then I could figure out how to fix it and Mr. Hefner would find out what I was really good for.

Fluffs of cotton scattered across the floors like dust balls under Granddaddy's bed. The big, high windows sent slants of light toward the spinning machines, and in those slants, bits of lint hovered in the air like they were looking for a landing place. Mostly it felt like the lint was settling in my eyeballs and sneaking into my nose and throat every time I took a breath. My head felt as if it was spinning faster than those frames.

I needed the open air of the woods with sunlight slanting through the trees. I wanted the racket to fade away and a woodpecker to take up the rhythm of the machines.

I tried to work faster. But the threads tangled and I had to straighten them out and that just slowed everything down. It seemed like Jake was flying up and down the row, changing out spools. A woman would come by with an empty cart for him and take away the one he'd just filled. She'd replace my carts too, but I wasn't filling them near fast enough.

Somehow I survived the day, but by the end of it, I was fit for the loony bin. I couldn't wait to be outside where I could breathe right and didn't have all that racket knocking around in my ears.

I went to see Mr. Hefner in his office like he told me to. "Junior, I observed you today," he said. "You're a good worker. You're not fast. Not yet. But you'll improve. How did you like it?"

Like it? Was it possible for someone to like being a doffer? "Uh. Uh . . ." I felt as if all the lint in that place had coated my tongue and my brain too. How was I going to answer him?

Mr. Hefner didn't wait. He just reached into his pocket and pulled out a dollar. "Here's your wages." He laid the dollar on his desk and nodded for me to take it. "Within sixty days half our production will be war work. Uniform fabric and such. And on June first, three of my doffers are going into the armed forces. You come back in two weeks and I just might have a job for you. If you still want it." He stood then. "And now I have other work to do."

Mr. Hefner was ready to have me out of his office. And boy howdy, was I ready to leave. I was fixing to go home, grab my gun, and head off into the woods where I could hear myself think. And sneeze the cotton dust out of my head.

38

BLUNDER
May 1942

Leroy was sitting in his truck across the street at Stewart Elrod's gas station. I climbed in, pulled the door shut, and rode out of Brookford with my eyes closed. Just behind my eyelids I could still see a thousand spinning spools of white.

As Leroy's truck picked up speed I leaned my head against the doorframe and let the wind hit me in the face, blowing my hair and clearing my nostrils.

"How'd it go?" asked Leroy.

I just shook my head. He didn't push me for an answer, and I never gave him one. He dropped me off at my mailbox. As soon as he drove away, I pulled off my shoes and socks. I needed to feel dirt on the bottoms of my feet.

Eleanor was already bawling and I knew there was gardening to do. There wouldn't be time for going into the woods. I tended the animals, and on the way back to the house I plopped myself down onto a sweet potato crate under Pop's big oak tree. I hadn't managed to rake up the acorns last fall, and one of them had sprouted into a small tree not four feet away.

It was only six inches high, but it had four perfect leaves and was doing its best to become a real tree. Any other time I would've pulled up a sprout like that. Today, though, I didn't have the heart to destroy it. After all, what if the big oak tree was hit by lightning one day? The seedling would be there to replace it.

I leaned my elbows on my knees and dropped my head in my hands and ran my fingers through my hair. When I did, bits of cotton jammed up under my fingernails. After supper I'd fill the washtub with warm soapy water and wash all the lint away. But for now, I just sat under that oak tree and thanked the good Lord that Pop had gotten himself out of Brookford and raised me up at the foot of Bakers Mountain.

The next morning I went back to doing what Pop would do if he was still alive, looking for fix-it jobs with neighboring farmers.

Garland Abernethy said he had a tree go down in a lightning storm. I could have it for firewood if I cut it up and hauled it off. It was too hot to be thinking about firewood, but I knew that, come winter, we'd be glad for it. So I hitched Grover to the wagon and spent two whole days sawing and chopping that tree.

On Saturday morning I was planning to take the wagon back over for the last load of wood when I realized that one of the wheels was broken. I knew how to fix a lot of things, but I wasn't going to work on that without the help of someone who'd done it before.

I thought about asking Leroy if I could borrow his truck. That didn't seem likely, though. The government was about to start rationing gas and nobody was making trips they didn't have to anymore.

Still, I needed that wood and Garland's farm was less than a mile away. I decided to walk down to Leroy's and see what he had to say about it.

He was in the garden. Ann Fay was there too, helping him pick peas. "Garden looks good," I said. "My peas aren't ready yet."

"Daddy put his peas in back in February," said Ann Fay.

"Back in February I was in school. Leroy, could I ask a favor?"

"What's that?"

"I've been hauling firewood from Garland Abernethy's place. My wagon wheel is broke. If you let me use your truck, I'll share some of the wood with you."

"Hmm," said Leroy. "It's a mite low on oil, but if you don't go farther than Garland's place, it should be okay."

"I have a can of motor oil in Pop's shed," I told him. "What about if I put that in before I go anywhere?"

Leroy nodded. "That'll be mighty fine," he said.

So I took the truck and headed up the road. Before I reached my lane, I saw Dudley walking down the road toward my mailbox. I decided this was my chance to show him I could drive too, so I turned and went up the road to meet him. I pulled alongside him. "Want a ride?"

He hopped in. "Whose truck?"

"Neighbor's. I'm hauling wood. Wanna help?"

He shrugged. "Not as good as swimming, but okay. We'll swim when we're done."

With the two of us working, we loaded up that wood in short order and headed back out Garland's lane. On the highway, just before Huffman Farm Road, Dudley told me to hang a right.

"What?"

"Turn here. I got a swimming hole to take you to."

I pulled over to the side of the road. "It's not my truck, Dudley. I can't just take it all over the countryside. And besides that, the government is fixing to announce a ration on gas."

"Just turn, Bledsoe." Dudley had his shirt off and he used it to wipe the sweat off his neck and chest. "The whole reason I sweated buckets to help you out was so we could swim afterwards. Come on. It's just down the road a piece."

Dudley didn't have to tell me it was hot. His armpits were stinking up the truck. I sat there looking at him, trying to make up my mind. According to what Ann Fay said, he'd taken a licking for going to Hog Hill with me. And he never even mentioned it. I guessed I owed him something for that.

So I turned and I drove around that curvy road till I

came to the intersection. I knew how to get to the river from there, but he told me to keep on going. "I found a spot with a rope swing. And a deep hole for jumping into."

"I sure hope Leroy isn't needing this truck," I told him.

We parked the truck near a small bridge and I followed him down to the water. Dudley took me upstream to a deep section he knew about. It was a good swimming hole for sure. The rope swing was long and smooth riding. And the drop into the water was perfect. I almost forgot about Leroy's truck sitting up there. We must've swum for about an hour before it hit me how much time had gone by. "We gotta go," I said.

We hurried back to the truck and headed toward home. Before we got to the main highway I heard some knocking sounds coming from under the hood. That's when I remembered about the oil.

Here I was, almost a mile from home, in a place I was not supposed to be, with this truck and no oil. How was I going to tell Leroy I forgot to put it in? I slammed my fists against the steering wheel and said some words that could bring on a sermon from Reverend Price. "Dudley!" I yelled. "Look what you made me do."

"What?"

"I promised Leroy I'd put oil in the truck and you came along and distracted me. The engine'll be ruined."

"Whoa! *You* forget to put oil in and it's *my* fault? I ain't taking the blame for that."

I knew it was all my doing. I could see Pop with the dipstick in his hand that first day when Leroy brought the truck by the house. *Oil looks okay now,* Pop had told Leroy. *But keep an eye on it or you'll be rebuilding the engine for sure.*

I pulled over to the side of the road. "I've got to have this truck towed."

"Naw. That's just the valves clattering. You can make it the rest of the way. Trust me. My daddy outran the cops with his valves a-clacking and he didn't kill the engine."

Something about that story didn't seem quite right. Wayne Walker was probably drunk when he told it. Or maybe he just straight-up lied to sound bigger than he was. But the truth was, I wanted to believe it. I wanted to believe I could make it back to my house and get to that can of Quaker State motor oil in Pop's shed. So I eased the truck back onto the road and headed toward home. I listened real close and drove real slow.

"You don't have to poke," said Dudley. "My old man was going eighty miles an hour with cops on his tail. His engine didn't blow."

"I'm not your old man," I said. "And the last thing I need is a cop on my tail."

"Maybe it's better if you go faster."

"Maybe it's better if you shut up."

We made it to the highway, and now we were a half mile from the turnoff to my house. I kept my ears tuned to the clattering of the valves.

"Keep your ears open," I told Dudley. "If you hear anything different, let me know."

"I thought you wanted me to shut up."

I didn't answer him. The boy could sure be aggravating. We turned off the highway by the Hinkle sisters' house, and when we did, the sound changed. *Now*, I heard more than a clattering—there was a loud popping sound. And just like that, the engine died.

39

HUMILIATED
May 1942

Turned out Miss Hinkle was heading for her mailbox. She stopped in her tracks for a minute and then hurried over to the door of Leroy's truck. She had her teacher face on. Suspicious.

"Junior. Dudley. Are you up to something?"

"No, ma'am," I said. "Leroy's truck quit."

"Does he know you have his truck?"

What did she think? That I would take it without asking?

"Wait a minute while I get the car keys," she said. "I'll give you boys a ride down to Leroy's house."

"It's okay," I said. "We can walk."

"I insist." Miss Pauline turned and started back toward her house.

"Let's go," said Dudley. "We don't need her help." We jumped out of the truck and started walking fast down the road, but we hadn't made it halfway to my mailbox when I heard her coming behind us.

"Hurry!" I told Dudley. "Through the cornfield."

We took off running toward Leroy's house. The corn wasn't even knee high, so we sure couldn't hide in there. But we ran anyhow. I was in plenty of trouble already, and I sure didn't need Miss Hinkle adding to it.

Well, it was too late for that. By the time we reached Leroy's she was waiting for us.

She stood in the Honeycutts' yard and listened while I blurted out what I'd done. How I saw Dudley coming and forgot to put the oil in, how we went a little bit out of our way, and I hoped I was wrong, but I thought I might've just ruined the engine.

Leroy didn't yell at me. I wished he would. He just set his jaw so tight I thought he might never open his mouth again. Miss Pauline did plenty of talking, though. And what she said made things even worse.

"I received a phone call just this morning from Buster Smith. He said that last Friday night these boys were seen all the way over at Hog Hill." She stopped and looked at Dudley, then at me. "In *my* car."

Out of the corner of my eye I could see the sweat dripping from Dudley's face into the dirt. I was sure sweating too. As far as I could tell, this would be a real good time for the world to come to an end.

"And now," said Miss Pauline. "You boys will take another ride in my car. This time, you'll be visiting your parents to tell them just what you've been up to."

So she and Leroy got into the front of her car, and

me and Dudley climbed into the back seat, and we all headed toward my house. "I was wondering why my car smelled of cigarettes," said Miss Pauline. "Then Buster called and everything made sense. I don't suppose you boys know where our spare key is?"

"I sure don't know," said Dudley.

"Junior?" said Miss Pauline.

I didn't see how I could wiggle out of this. "Uh. Uh. Did you look under the furniture on the porch?"

"Yes, we certainly did. But that was on Friday afternoon. Before the car was taken. Maybe I should look again?"

"Maybe," I said.

Miss Pauline nodded just a little, but she didn't say a word.

There were three cars in our lane—Momma's sewing circle friends, who just happened to be sitting on the front porch knitting socks and scarves to send to soldiers. I couldn't have picked a worse time to get myself into a heap of trouble.

Miss Pauline and Leroy looked at each other, and I could see they were trying to decide whether to teach me a lesson in front of those women. But I also knew they hated the idea of shaming Momma.

"We'll call Bessie aside," said Leroy. "Let's go, boys."

Momma smiled and waved when she saw Miss Pauline and Leroy getting out of the car. But that smile shriveled up like a slice of dried apple by the time we reached the porch. I reckoned she could tell from the hang of my head I'd done something real bad.

Leroy tipped his hat. "Good afternoon, ladies. Reckon we could have a word with Bessie?"

Lottie Scronce gathered her yarn and Mrs. Basil Whitener did too. Mildred Rhinehart said, "We'll wait inside."

Momma watched them go, and then it was like she changed her mind about them disappearing. Maybe she wanted her friends around her when she heard the bad news. Or, more likely, she wanted me to learn a lesson right in front of them. Because she stood and let the yarn on her lap fall to the porch floor. "Come inside," she said. She shook her finger at me. "Junior, hold that door like a real gentleman."

I bolted up the steps and opened the screen door. Once we were inside, it was like Momma turned into an army sergeant, the way she told Miss Pauline where to sit and me and Dudley to stand right there by the door and wait. Then she went into the kitchen. I could see the women in there—more than just the ones who'd been on the porch. Some were working at the kitchen table, turning bed sheets into bandages.

Momma brought every last one of them into the living room. They filed in, looking confused and a little nervous. Some of them carried bandages. As if they'd need them to treat the wounded.

They filled the sofa and chairs and Momma stood in

the kitchen doorway. Leroy was pacing in front of the fireplace. I couldn't help but notice his hands were curled into fists. "Junior. You have some explaining to do."

"Yes, sir." I didn't look at Momma. Or the rest of those women. I just couldn't. I stuttered around until finally I pushed the words past the knot in my throat. "Leroy let me use his truck, and I promised to put oil in it. But after I left Garland's place we went to the river for a quick swim. I reckon I forgot about the oil."

"Heaven help us," said Momma. I could tell she hoped it wasn't what she thought it was. But she couldn't live with Pop for all those years and not know things about cars—whether she wanted to or not.

"The engine went out."

Momma gasped. "Have mercy, Junior!" The words came out of her like a shot from a 12-gauge. She grabbed ahold of the doorjamb.

Lottie Scronce got up from her chair and took Momma by the arm. "You sit down, Bessie." Momma kind of sagged into the armchair just a few feet away from me.

My mind was scrambling for some way to make this all better. "I'll pay for it, Momma. Don't you worry. Mr. Hefner said I can work at the mill if I want to. I'll be a doffer. I learned how to do that."

Momma sat there with both hands over her mouth. "Have mercy," she said again. Only this time the words were muffled.

I wanted to tell everybody, including Dudley, to go away and leave me there with just Momma so I could convince her that everything would be okay. But the truth was, she hadn't heard the half of it, and the next part was going to be even harder than the first.

Miss Pauline spoke up then. "I'm sorry, Bessie. But I'm afraid there's more. Junior, tell her what else you did."

The living room turned so quiet that all I could hear was the ticking of the clock on the mantel. I snuck a peek at Momma. Her hands were still over her mouth like they were stuck there. And her eyes—I saw the fear in them. Because she knew, as bad as things were, they were about to be worse.

"We . . . I mean, I. I wanted to know about Pop and what happened that night. I meant it for good, Momma. Honest, I did. I don't know why we borrowed the Hinkle sisters' car without asking. I don't know what got into me."

I started going on and on, talking too much, trying to explain that I didn't mean to be bad. I wanted to be a man and take care of her, but somehow it was like ever since Pop died, everything was so mixed up inside.

Momma was sitting in that same chair where she sat the night the deputy came. Only thing was, when she learned about Pop dying, she held herself together. When I told her about me stealing Miss Pauline's car, she fell all to pieces.

While she sat there crying, I kept saying, "I'm sorry, Momma. I'm sorry. I'll make it right with Leroy and Miss Pauline. I'll make it up to you. I didn't mean to shame you, Momma."

"Shame *me?*" said Momma. She sat up stiff as Miss Pauline and looked at me. "The person you have just shamed in front of the whole community, Axel Bledsoe, Junior, is your own self. And if you want to make it up to anybody, *that* is who you need to make it up to. Look at these women." She waved her arm in a big circle that took in the whole room.

Momma waited while I worked up my courage to glance around the room. Her friends sat—every one of them on the edge of their seat—staring at me.

"These are your witnesses, Junior. They will be watching while you earn yourself some respect."

"Yes, ma'am," I said. Standing there, full of shame, I realized something for the first time. Respect wasn't something another person could take away from me or Momma. Those women knew that Pop was a drunk. But that didn't change who Momma was. They'd respected her all along.

They could respect *me* again, too, even though right that minute it didn't seem likely. But *I* was the only one who could earn it.

40

GRANDDADDY
May 1942

"Rise and shine, Junior!" That was Momma calling from the kitchen. I pulled myself up out of sleep, but I didn't want to face Monday morning. All night I'd dreamed about that truck sitting by the side of the road. And spools of white thread spinning and clacking in my head.

I wasn't sure I could make it through even a week of being a doffer. Just the thought of chasing those spools around and breathing in all that lint made me want to lock myself in my room with Granddaddy.

But Momma had told Leroy and Miss Pauline they could punish me as they saw fit. Leroy had said he sure hated to do this, but he thought it only right that I should pay for it. Jerm Foster could do the repairs.

You would think a schoolteacher would have plenty of punishment tricks up her sleeve, but Miss Pauline wanted time to think of a fitting consequence. I was supposed to talk to her and Miss Dinah about that today, as soon as Miss Pauline came home from school.

"Junior!" Momma called again.

For some reason Granddaddy's radio was off and he was still in bed. I pulled on my britches and then my shirt, and while I was buttoning it up I noticed something. Granddaddy sure was quiet. He wasn't snoring, not even a little bit. And I didn't hear him breathing.

I stopped buttoning my shirt and stared. His mouth hung open like he'd been caught in the middle of a snore. His eyes were shut, and he wasn't moving. His left arm hung off the side of the bed, so I picked it up, and sure enough, it was cold. I placed it across his stomach.

The feel of his body with no life—it hit me like a Judgment Day sermon from Reverend Price. Granddaddy had been in my room for close on a year now, and I'd spent most of that time wishing he was someplace else. Wishing he'd be quiet.

And now he was.

"Momma!" I yelled. "It's Granddaddy. I think he's dead."

She came running. She wiped her hands on her apron and put them on his forehead like she was checking for a fever, then shook her head real slow. She turned to me. "Run up to the Hinkle sisters' and call Dr. Johnson."

I finished buttoning my shirt while I went out the door, and I combed my hair with my fingers on the way up the road. Then I thought, *What in the world is the big hurry? He's gone, and rushing won't bring him back.* So I slowed down and caught my breath and tried not to think about whether I was sorry or relieved.

That silly song went through my head. *He went to bed and he bumped his head and didn't wake up in the morning.*

Miss Dinah was outside in the vegetable garden. "Could I use your telephone?" I asked.

"Well, good morning, Junior."

"Good morning, Miss Dinah. I didn't mean to be rude."

"Is everything all right?"

I shook my head. "It's Granddaddy. He's dead. I need to call Dr. Johnson."

Miss Dinah gasped. "Dear me," she said. She started peeling off her garden gloves. "You go ahead and use the phone, Junior. I'll be right in."

I went through the back porch and there was Miss Pauline cleaning up the breakfast dishes. "Why, Junior!" she said. "What brings you here?"

"Miss Dinah said I could come in. Granddaddy's dead and I need to use the telephone. If you don't mind."

"Of course." Miss Pauline motioned toward the living room, but I knew right where the telephone was since I'd used it plenty of times. I'd memorized Dr. Johnson's number, too. I called and he promised to arrange for a coroner to pick up the body.

Before I was off the phone, I heard Miss Dinah come inside and wash her hands.

"Sit," she said, pointing to the kitchen table. She pulled three small glasses down from the cupboard. Then she reached into her Frigidaire for a bottle of Cheerwine. She divided it between the glasses and handed one to me.

Miss Pauline fussed. "Cheerwine at this time of day! What are you thinking, Dinah?"

"I am thinking Junior needs a little cheer. There's no law saying a body can't enjoy a soda at six-thirty in the morning."

Miss Pauline pushed her glass to me and poured herself a cup of tea. It was real quiet while we had our drinks. I reckon none of us knew what to say. But I owed them an apology. Finally I worked up my courage.

"Miss Dinah. Miss Pauline. I'm real sorry about stealing your car. I'll make it up to you. I promise. I'll work your garden or fix things around here. Or whatever you say."

Miss Pauline set her teacup in its saucer. "Whatever I say?"

"Yes, ma'am."

"Well then, Junior. I have given this much consideration, and what I want is for you to go back to school."

Back to school? I'd have to do ninth grade all over again. And Miss Hinkle would be my teacher.

It was like she could read my mind. "I'm retiring for certain," she said. "However, before I do, I believe I can persuade Mr. Hollar to let you move forward with your class. After you catch up, of course."

"But school is almost over."

"You aren't done with me yet, Junior. I'll expect you

255

to sit at this table every weekday for two hours all summer long. Maybe if I don't have any other students and you don't have any distractions you can keep your mind on your work. Do we have an agreement?"

I thought about her offer. I imagined holding my pencil in my right hand and struggling to make my letters lean in the right direction. I could hear Miss Hinkle's voice now, droning away. *Do not fail to see and correct all errors.*

I didn't know when I could find two hours a day for schooling. I would have to work at the mill to pay Jerm for fixing the truck. And of course I had the garden and other chores.

But my mistakes were staring me in the face, and I had to fix them. At least I wouldn't have time for getting into trouble with Dudley Walker.

Before I left there, I promised to go back to school. The Hinkle sisters told me I was forgiven, and I should tell Dudley to come by and make things right with them too.

41

POP'S FAMILY
May 1942

Miss Pauline went into school late that day just so she could drive Momma and me to Brookford to break the news to Pop's sisters.

Aunt Lillian was wearing a housecoat when she opened the door. And her brown hair was smashed into funny shapes, as if she'd just climbed out of bed.

"Dear me," she said, flapping her hands and talking real fast. "I'm not exactly ready for company."

"I'm sorry to barge in," said Momma, "but—Hammer died this morning."

"Hammer? Dead?" Aunt Lillian threw both hands over her mouth and just stood there and wailed. "Oh, dear. Daddy's actually gone? I was planning on visiting him this summer." She flapped her hands some more. "Did you tell Lucy?"

Momma shook her head. "Not yet."

"We have to tell her." Lillian pushed right past us and marched across the yard with her blue housecoat flowing out behind her. "Lucy, oh, poor Lucy. What will we ever do?"

Momma stood there for a minute, shaking her head. "Reckon how Lucille will take the news? Pull the door shut, Junior."

Lillian had left the door standing wide open and what I saw inside was a regular junkyard. The living room was overloaded with furniture and all sorts of things. Tools. Boxes of dishes. Even a spinning wheel. A body could hardly walk through it.

"Lord, have mercy," said Momma. "That right there explains why Hammer's house was empty when we picked him up. Lillian has stuffed all his and Granny's things in here. Let's go, Junior."

When we got to Lucille's, she had just opened the door for Lillian. "Sakes alive, Lillian! Why are *you* here?" I bet the two of them hadn't spoken to each other since the last time I was there. And this time Lillian hadn't brought fudge to bribe her sister.

When Aunt Lucille caught sight of *us* on her porch, she grabbed onto Lillian. "Oh, dear. Is Daddy all right?"

"Noooooo!" wailed Lillian. She threw herself into her sister's arms. "Oh, Lucy, what will we ever do without him?"

Lucille pulled Lillian into the house and we followed. The two of them sank onto the sofa and cried onto each other's shoulders.

If they cared so cotton-pickin' much, why couldn't they have realized it sooner?

Momma pulled a side chair up close to them. Every so often she'd say, "I'm sorry, Lillian. I'm sorry, Lucille." As if it was all her fault. "We didn't have any idea he was about to go. Dr. Johnson said most likely his heart just gave out."

"He always did have a bad heart," said Aunt Lucille. "Oh, poor Daddy. We'll miss him so."

"But we thought you didn't care," said Momma. "Why didn't you visit?"

Aunt Lillian dabbed at her eyes. "He was always yelling, wasn't he, Lucy?" She sounded frightened. "Why was he always yelling?"

Aunt Lucille patted Lillian's shoulder. She looked at Momma and explained. "Our poor dear mother—God rest her soul—she said life had dealt Daddy a bad hand and people should be kind to him."

"We tried," said Lillian. "When Mother passed, we tried to take care of him. But we could never be good enough. My fudge was too soft." Lillian started bawling all over again.

"I didn't get the grease stain out of his shirt," said Lucille. "Land's sake, it had been there two years! Mother couldn't wash it out either, so why did he throw a cup at me?" Her lip trembled and she rubbed at a scar on her chin.

"Have mercy," said Momma. "No wonder Axel and Hammer couldn't be in the same room."

When she said that, the aunts pulled apart, turning stiff as two mailboxes standing by the highway. Lucille's face went slack, and she stared at the flowered rug on the floor. When she spoke, it was real slow and quiet.

"Lily," she said, "remember when you dropped the dipper in the well and you didn't own up to it? Daddy beat Axel until he couldn't sit down." Lucille shivered and hugged herself. "I can still hear how he whimpered all night long."

Momma moaned. She was hurting for Pop and I was too. I could almost feel that licking. And something told me Pop had felt it up until that night on Hog Hill. When finally his heart just gave out.

Aunt Lillian turned and pointed her finger at Lucille, jabbing the air between them. "Oh, and *you're* so upstanding. Remember when you lied about breaking that window? Axel took a beating for that, too. Just because he had a new bat."

Those two sisters threw their tales back and forth like baseballs they couldn't wait to get rid of. And neither one of them was catching what got thrown at her.

But I sure was. And Momma was too. Finally she said, "Lord, have mercy! I'm just so sorry for every one of you. Please, no more stories!"

From the sound of things, everybody in Hammer

Bledsoe's family had a lifetime of hatefulness weighing them down. The aunts were each trying to prove they had the worse end of the deal. But if you asked me, Pop was the one who suffered most.

That's why he never took a belt or a hickory stick to me. Somewhere along the way he must have decided he wasn't going to pass the meanness down the line. In my mind's eye, I saw him walking up that hill and out of Brookford with only the clothes on his back, and maybe a wrench in his hip pocket. Determined to find his own way in the world.

42

REPAIR
May 1942

Momma packed up every last stitch of Granddaddy's clothing, all his newspaper clippings, and the Theodore Roosevelt poster, and set them by the door. She told me to carry Granddaddy's chair to the front porch. "In case those sisters come popping in and want it all back."

"What about the radio?" I asked.

"I'm putting my foot down on that one. Both of those women have a radio already, and we need to keep up with war news. So do the Honeycutts."

I washed Granddaddy's filthy spitting can and set it in a pasteboard box with other metal we were collecting for the war effort. He had ten empty Skoal tins and one half-full one. I put them in the box too.

Momma scrubbed my room down with pine oil and we pushed the bed to the opposite wall from where it was. She even pulled a different quilt out of her cedar chest and put it on my bed. The place looked and smelled like a whole new room. And something about that made me think I could have a new start on life.

I set the photograph of Gideon Bledsoe on the table by my bed and tried to imagine what he'd say if he was standing there in front of me. But maybe I didn't need him to say a word. Maybe his kind eyes said it all—not to let hard times turn me mean.

I still had to get Leroy's truck fixed, so I climbed on Grover and headed into Brookford. After talking to Jerm, I'd ride to the mill to tell Mr. Hefner I wanted the doffer job. Only thing was, I *didn't* want it. My eyes burned just thinking about all that lint. I doubted I could live through one more day in that place, but I'd made a mess of things and fixing that mess was going to take money.

Jerm was flat on his back under a car. He shimmied out from under and sat up. "Junior. I'm real sorry to hear about Hammer's passing. When is the service?"

"Whenever the aunts decide."

Jerm chuckled. "You mean, whenever they can agree. That could take a while. Anything I can do?"

"Well, sir, I reckon I have a job for you."

"How's that?"

"I blew the engine in Leroy Honeycutt's truck."

Jerm let out a long whistle. "That '35 Chevrolet?"

"I'll work in the mill to pay for it. Could you start on it soon as possible?"

"You sure Leroy wants me to do it? How come he's not the one asking?"

"He said he'd stop in after work. But first, I reckon he wanted me to confess my own sins."

Jerm cocked his head and gave me a questioning look.

"He loaned me the truck and I was supposed to put oil in it. But I kind of got sidetracked."

Jerm wiped his greasy hands on a rag. Then he flapped that rag toward my face in a friendly way. "Aren't you Axel Bledsoe's boy? And didn't Axel have a block and tackle?"

"Yes, sir. It's still there."

Jerm clapped my shoulder. "You know Otis Hickey." He pointed back up the road. "If I'm not mistaken, he has an engine in his scrapyard out back that'll have some parts you need, likely some pistons and maybe some rods. You'll save some money and do Axel Bledsoe proud at the same time."

I never did make it to the mill to take that job. Jerm left that car he was repairing, and we headed up to see Otis, whose place was just about as junky in the front as it was around back. Jerm knocked on the door, and Otis came out squinting against the daylight.

"Morning, Otis," said Jerm. He told him what we wanted, and Otis took us around to see the engine. Jerm did some bartering with him and said he'd come again later, after he took a look at Leroy's truck. Then we headed back down the hill.

"I'll have to order some of the parts," said Jerm. "But first I need to see how Leroy feels about our plan."

"Yes, sir," I said.

I spent the rest of the day working around the house,

bending over backwards to please Momma. That evening, when I was cutting the grass, I looked up and there was a truck coming up the lane. It was Basil Whitener, who Leroy had been catching a ride with, and he was towing Leroy's truck behind him.

I left my grass cutter in the front yard and headed around to the back. Leroy was unhooking the chain between the two trucks. "We stopped in at the garage," he said. "Jerm told me what the two of you had cooked up."

"You okay with that, Leroy?"

"Long as Jerm backs us up."

Leroy was ready to start working. So we used Pop's block and tackle to pull the engine and lower it onto a tarpaulin there in the yard. Basil stuck around to help that first night, and Jerm showed up the next day with parts, bringing Otis Hickey along with him.

"You're looking at a soldier man," said Otis, poking himself in the chest. "Uncle Sam has picked my number."

And that right there made the war feel real close. It didn't hit me the way it would if Leroy was leaving us. But still, Otis was the one who'd stood on that swinging bridge and told me things about Pop I would never know otherwise.

While we worked on that truck, he filled our ears with more stories—about him and Pop walking across the Brookford dam when they were boys. About Pop's sisters being so frightened of that bridge they tried crossing it on their hands and knees. "But they still couldn't do it," he said. "Some people are just scared. Ain't nothing going to convince them to cross over."

I hated to see those fellows leave when it started getting dark of an evening. I wanted to stay under that oak tree, changing out pistons and adjusting spark plugs. Enjoying the sound of Jerm Foster's laugh and Leroy putting in his two cents every once in a while. Having them there felt a little bit like having Pop back. Except nobody was singing "Amazing Grace" and *I* actually got my hands in the grease.

On Friday night, when it was all done, Leroy reached in his pocket and pulled out the key. "Put some oil in this truck and you can be the first to drive it."

And if that right there wasn't amazing, I didn't know what was. I went into Pop's shed and poked around on the shelves until I found the Quaker State motor oil. I could hear the men out there under the oak tree tossing wrenches into their toolboxes. I liked the sound of their deep voices, but I wasn't in a hurry to leave the dusty, oily smells inside the shed.

"Pop," I whispered. "I sure do miss you. Even if you were a wretch sometimes. At least you were a better wretch than Granddaddy was. And I aim to do better than you and him both. I've got Leroy and the others to keep me on the straight and narrow."

43

TURN AROUND
May 1942

On Saturday morning I found Dudley at the river with his fishing pole and a string full of catfish dangling in the water.

"Where's your pole?" he asked.

"I didn't come to go fishing."

"Suit yourself."

"My granddaddy died."

"Oh." Dudley stared at the water like he was looking in there for something to say. Finally he said, "I'm sorry."

I shrugged. "I got my bed back and it's quiet in my room now. He was a cantankerous old cuss, you know that?"

Dudley nodded.

"His whole family was ornery, but I reckon he made 'em that way. His heart gave out. Just like my pop's did."

"Must run in the family," said Dudley. And then it was like he realized what he'd just said. "Course that don't mean it'll happen to you."

"Not if I can help it. I don't know what makes a

body's heart give out. But I decided some things, Dudley, and I'm here to tell you about 'em."

"Shoot."

"I'm not going to be like them. Pop could be ornery too, and I reckon I don't blame him on account of how Granddaddy treated him. He probably did the best he could. I know he aimed to be a better father than his daddy was. He did all right until he started drinking."

I sat down on the bank beside Dudley. "I know one thing. I won't be spending my life running to Hog Hill or some other dead-end place the way Pop did. I'm going to do something different. I'll be upstanding, is what I'll be. Just so you know, I won't be stealing cars or letting you talk me into doing stupid things. You hear?"

"I'm listening."

"Good. And another thing. You have to go see Miss Hinkle. And her sister, Miss Dinah. You owe them a big 'I'm sorry.'"

Dudley frowned. And he said a few bad words.

"You can handle it. But don't be surprised what kind of punishment they give you. Miss Hinkle roped me into taking ninth grade all over again—at her kitchen table. So I can go on to tenth grade next year."

"Yee haw!" said Dudley. He gave my shoulder a fistful of wallop.

"Hey! Just because we're in the same grade don't mean I'll be talking with the likes of you. Not unless you make things right with them first. I'm done with troublemaking, you hear?"

"You said that one time already."

"All right, then. Whatcha going to do about it?"

"Now? You want me to go now? What about my fish?"

"You can come back for them. Or, here's a better idea. Take them to Miss Pauline. Tell her you'll clean 'em for her."

Dudley hefted himself off the riverbank and gathered up his pole and the string of fish, and we headed back toward my house. It was about a mile and a half away. We passed Garland Abernethy's lane, and right about that time I saw something move in the side ditch. At first I thought it was a groundhog, but then I realized it was a dog.

"Well, I'll be a monkey's uncle."

"What?"

"It looks like Ann Fay Honeycutt just got herself a dog."

44

PETE
June 1942

I carried the little rat terrier in a cardboard box to the Honeycutts'. I went around to the back door, and sure enough, Leroy had the family working in the garden. Myrtle was tying up string beans, and Ann Fay was helping Leroy hoe weeds. Even the twins were dipping tin cans into a bucket and pouring water onto the tomato plants. The front of Ida's dress was drenched, and Ellie was drinking from her can.

"Hey," I said. "You don't look like a tomato plant to me."

Ellie giggled and poured the water on top of her head. It ran down past her ears and over her eyes. She blinked and the water splashed off her eyelashes.

I didn't blame her for drenching herself. I was wet too—soaked with sweat. June was always hot and sticky, but this year seemed worse than usual.

Out of the corner of my eye I saw Ann Fay drop her hoe and come running. "Hey, Junior. What's in that box?" She wiped at her face with her sleeve.

"It's a surprise." I carried the box over to the house and set it up on the porch floor. Bobby was there on a crazy quilt, sleeping with only his diaper on. "Are you ready?"

Ann Fay jumped up onto the porch and lifted one of the flaps on the box. "A dog?" She said it so quietly it sounded almost like she was whispering a prayer. Then she squealed. "It's a dog. Where'd you get him, Junior?"

The pup scooted into the corner of the box and whimpered.

"Shh. You're scaring him. He was in the side ditch. Someone dropped him off, I reckon."

Ann Fay jumped off the porch and headed back to the garden. "Daddy! Come look what Junior brought." She grabbed Leroy's arm, which was moving back and forth because he was hoeing, but she hung on and didn't give up. "Come, Daddy."

Leroy loved his garden, that's one thing for sure. But evidently he loved Ann Fay even more. He let her drag him toward the house, stepping over rows of beans and winding through the tomato plants. Myrtle straightened up from the beans and stood there rubbing the small of her back, groaning just a little. Then she left her bushel basket and followed Leroy and Ann Fay.

I had the pup in my arms by this time, and he was snuggled into me like that would protect him from these strangers. I scooted my backside up onto the edge of the porch. Ida plopped down beside me and held out her hands. "I want to hold it."

"No. Let me hold it." Ellie poked the dog's belly with her finger.

Leroy took off his straw hat and slapped it against the porch post. Then he plopped it on Ann Fay's head. She grinned and pulled it down over her ears.

"What you got there, Junior?" asked Leroy.

"Well, sir, it's not a cat. And it's not a cow. So it must be a dog."

"Can we keep him, Daddy? Puhleaze." Ann Fay tugged on Leroy's arm.

The girl could learn a thing or two about giving a man a little peace and quiet. I wanted to tell her to hush and leave him alone or she'd ruin the whole thing.

Leroy frowned. "I don't need another mouth to feed."

"Poor stray needs a family," I said. "And we have two dogs already."

"Here, Junior. Let me hold him." Ann Fay didn't wait for me to hand him over. Just took him right out of my arms. But the first thing he did was leap onto the porch and run off. When he came to the crazy quilt he stopped and sniffed all around Bobby. Then he licked his fist.

Myrtle frowned and started to reach for her baby boy, but the dog curled right up next to him like somehow that young'un would protect him.

"Daddy, look," said Ann Fay. "He likes the baby. Poor little puppy needs someone to love. We'll take good care of him, Daddy. He'll make me real happy, Daddy."

Leroy sighed and shook his head. He looked at Ann

Fay and I saw a little grin growing on his face. "Junior Bledsoe, what have you done to me?"

I knew then that he was giving in.

Ann Fay grabbed my elbow. "What's his name?"

I shrugged her off. "Like I said, I found him by the side of the road. He didn't come with a sign announcing his name, for Pete's sake."

"Pete!" yelled Ida. "We'll call him Pete."

Seemed like everybody else in the family just stood there nodding.

Pete was all snuggled up against that baby boy, and now he had his head on the child's belly. When Bobby breathed, it was like he was rocking that little dog's head. Up and down. Up and down.

Leroy started to draw water from the well and Myrtle fetched cups from the kitchen and we sat on the edge of the porch and in the grass and drank clean, cold water. I told them about Aunt Lily dropping the dipper into the well and how Pop took a licking for it.

"That's not fair!" said Ann Fay.

"Sounds like he took a lot of whuppings he didn't deserve," I said.

I thought how it was going on a year since my pop had died. An awful lot had happened since then. The Japs had attacked Pearl Harbor and now we were at war.

If the war went on long enough, Leroy Honeycutt still might have to go off to fight.

I sure hoped not. If it wasn't for him and a few others,

even Miss Pauline, I'd probably still be stumbling around making a mess of myself.

One thing for sure, if Leroy did get drafted, I aimed to help look after Ann Fay and the rest of the family—just the way he'd always looked after me.

Nobody could take the place of their daddy. I knew that as well as anybody. But I could help with the garden and fix just about anything that broke. And I'd do my level best to be as steady and upstanding as the porch post I was leaning against right that minute.

EPILOGUE

Maybe me and Pop don't go together
    like biscuits and gravy
the way Ann Fay and Leroy do.
But according to Granddaddy
the acorn didn't fall far from the tree.

I reckon I do have some of Pop's ways
    about me,
and he had some good ones, for sure—
how he loved my momma
and the way he got along with his
    neighbors, real good.
He had a heart as big as Bakers
    Mountain
And a knack for fixing whatever
    broke—
not for money, but just for the love of
    doing it.
Those are the things I'm aiming for.

And when I feel like I'm up in the air
    on a scary bridge
I'll hang on to his words.
Don't look down.
Keep your eye on where you're going.
You'll get across just fine.

AUTHOR'S NOTE

When my publisher asked me to consider writing a prequel to *Blue*, I knew immediately that Junior Bledsoe would be the protagonist. Junior is one of my favorite characters from *Blue* and its sequel, *Comfort*. I love his neighborliness and the never-ending support he gave to Ann Fay Honeycutt during her family's hard times.

But I knew he hadn't always been so mature and that he had probably been shaped by his own difficulties. So I took a seed from *Blue* in which Ann Fay says, "Junior is seventeen years old. He's the man of his house too, ever since his daddy's heart give out a few years ago." From those lines grew a story about what had happened to Junior's father and how Junior responded to the challenges of losing him.

When I wrote *Blue* I had no idea of the dysfunction in Junior's family. But I've witnessed family dysfunction and wanted to explore the conflicting feelings that children experience in families that don't run smoothly.

BROOKFORD MILLS

It wasn't until Junior played hooky from school that I realized the mill town of Brookford would become a part of the story. As a child, I rode through Brookford on my way to Hickory and was always intrigued with the hills covered in tiny white houses, the mill, the dam, and the swinging bridge.

Brookford Mills was in operation from 1898 until the late 1950s. Farmers in neighboring communities grew cotton to supply the mill, and individuals like Junior helped pick it. In fact, local schools planned their schedules so that students would be free during cotton-picking season in September.

WHO WAS REAL? WHO WAS NOT?

Most of the characters in *Aim* are fictional. Some, however, were real. Jerm Foster was a Brookford resident with a reputation for being an upstanding citizen and a fine mechanic. Stewart Elrod ran the Brookford Service Station. Garland Abernethy was a farmer who lived in Junior's neighborhood.

Joe DiMaggio played baseball for the New York Yankees, and between May and July of 1941 he enjoyed the longest hitting streak in baseball history—fifty-six games. At a time when Americans were anxious about going to war, he served as an inspiration and a call to greatness. In the early 1940s, most major league baseball games were played during the day and recreated via telegrams for broadcasting on the radio.

Sergeant Alvin C. York was also a real person. His finely honed hunting skills gave him near-perfect aim. During World War I, in a battle in France, York used his sharpshooting skills to defeat the enemy, leading eight other Americans in capturing 132 German soldiers. For several decades York rejected offers to make his story into a motion picture. By the outbreak of World War II, however, he believed that such a movie could help protect innocent people from greedy dictators. Beginning in the summer of 1941, *Sergeant York* played in theaters nationwide, spurring patriotism and support for the war. York's photograph appeared several times in the *Hickory Daily Record* and in other publications across the country as part of the propaganda campaign to persuade Americans to get behind the war.

THE HOMEFRONT

By 1941, Germany, Italy, and Japan had allied themselves in their various military campaigns against innocent people. Americans who read the news were divided about whether to step in and help. Some felt the problems in Europe, Africa, and Asia belonged to the people who lived in those places and that we should stay out of the war altogether. Others were in favor of sending military equipment, but not our men, to the battlefield. On December 7, 1941, when Japan bombed the U.S. naval base at Pearl Harbor, public opinion immediately shifted. Americans now believed that the "Axis powers"—Japan, Italy, and Germany—were determined to eventually conquer North America.

Americans would not sit by and allow such a thing to happen. Citizens across the nation began to support the war effort, conserving resources, recycling items that could be used to produce armaments, buying war bonds, enlisting in the armed forces, and much more. As America's men went off to war, women took their places in jobs they would never have imagined. In addition to doing factory work and using heavy equipment, they built airplanes, battleships, and weapons. Many assisted the war effort on the battlefront, serving as army nurses and flying airplanes on non-combat missions.

World War II profoundly changed America. It produced a powerful sense of patriotism, rearranged attitudes toward women and racial minorities, and gave the average American a much greater sense of belonging to a world community.

RESOURCES

BOOKS

The Home Front: USA World War II, by Ronald H. Bailey
(Time Life Books, 1977)

My War: From Bismarck to Britain and Back, by Ruth Register
Coleman. (Trafford Publishing, 2006)

*Yesterday's Child: Growing Up in a Mill Town during
the Great Depression,* by Dorothy Sigmon Holbrook
(Catawba County Historical Association, 1998)

Brookford Memories, by Dyke Little (Watermark, 2010)

America at War, 1941–1945: The Home Front, by Clark G.
Reynolds (Gallery Books, 1990)

Sergeant York: His Own Life Story and War Diary, by Tom
Skeyhill (Doubleday, Doran and Co., 1928)

VIDEOS

America Goes to War: The Homefront WWII, by Eric Sevareid.
Washington, DC: PBS, Anthony Potter Productions, 1990.

Sergeant York, by Howard Hawks. Burbank, CA: Warner
Brothers Pictures, 2006.

The War, by Ken Burns and Lynn Novick. Washington, DC:
PBS, 2007.

WEBSITES OF INTEREST[*]
baseball-almanac.com/ (Baseball Almanac)

joedimaggio.com/ (Joe DiMaggio's official website)

Websites current at time of publication

acacia.pair.com/Acacia.Vignettes/The.Diary.of.Alvin.York.html (*The Diary of Alvin York*)

docs.fdrlibrary.marist.edu/091141.html (Fireside Chat 110, September 11, 1941, "On Maintaining Freedom of the Seas"—President Roosevelt's address to the nation after the USS *Greer* exchanged fire with a German U-boat)

docs.fdrlibrary.marist.edu/tmirhdee.html (December 8, 1941, President Roosevelt asks Congress for a Declaration of War)

docs.fdrlibrary.marist.edu/120941.html (Fireside Chat 140, December 9, 1941—President Roosevelt's address to the nation after Congress declares war on Japan)

BOOKS FOR YOUNG PEOPLE

Counting on Grace, by Elizabeth Winthrop (Wendy Lamb, 2006)

Early Sunday Morning: The Pearl Harbor Diary of Amber Billows, by Barry Denenberg (Scholastic, 2001)

Flygirl, by Sherri L. Smith (G.P. Putnam Sons Books for Young Readers, 2009)

Joe DiMaggio: Young Sports Hero, by Herb Dunn (Aladdin, 1999)

Kids at Work: Lewis Hine and the Crusade against Child Labor, by Russell Freedman and Lewis Wickes Hine (Clarion, 1994)

Lyddie, by Katherine Paterson (Lodestar, 1991)

Mare's War, by Tanita Davis (Knopf Books for Young Readers, 2009)

My Secret War: The World War II Diary of Madeline Beck, by Mary Pope Osborne (Scholastic, 2000)

Sergeant York, by John Perry (Thomas Nelson, 2010)

The Streak, by Barb Rosenstock (Calkins Creek Books, 2014)

The World Wars, by Paul Dowswell, Ruth Brocklehurst, and Henry Brook (Usborne Books, 2007)

World War II: Fighting for Freedom: The Story of the Conflict That Changed the World, 1934–1945, by Peter Chrisp (Scholastic, 2010)

THANK YOU!

I'm grateful to Carolyn Yoder who, more than a decade ago, suggested I research a story in my own backyard. That challenge led to the writing of *Blue*, which led to *Comfort*. Eventually, the publisher, Boyds Mills Press/Calkins Creek Books, asked for a prequel. *Aim* was born.

Thank you to Larry Mosteller and Ken Moyer for ensuring that my car scenes were accurate, to Andy and Naomi Bivens and Donna Ward for sharing their expertise concerning work in a cotton mill, to Rebecca Huffman for information about Mountain View High School in the 1940s, and to Robin Shelton, Pearl Davis, and Dyke Little for reflections on life in Brookford.

Thank you to Joanne Hunsberger for proofreading and Katya Rice for copyedits and to each person at Boyds Mills Press who helped to bring *Aim* to publication.

Kudos to my beta readers, Shannon Hitchcock, Wendy Hostetter Davis, Chuck Hostetter, Kay Mosteller, Gail and Abby Hickok, Mel Hager, Carol Baldwin, Judge Avery, and also to my writer friend Rebecka. I love that each of you read *Aim* while it was rough around the edges and helped me point it in the right direction.

BAKERS MOUNTAIN STORIES

At the foot of Bakers Mountain in western North Carolina lies a memorable family community where back-door friends are best and neighbors help each other through difficult times. In this series, set during the 1940s, 50s, and 60s, three families—the Honeycutts, the Bledsoes, and the Hinkle sisters—overcome personal hardships.

Trouble comes after all of them at one time or another, in the form of family dysfunction, disease, death, missteps, war, or postwar trauma. But these southerners are made of a grit that's as enduring as the red earth beneath their feet. And there is nothing so big that some home cooking, shared tears, and a helping hand can't fix.

The stories take place during a time when the country is experiencing dramatic social change. World War II takes women into the workplace, America begins to address its issues of racial inequality, and many fear communism as a threat to their way of life.

The stories are told by Ann Fay Honeycutt, her siblings, and their neighbor, Junior Bledsoe. They are tales about young teens coming of age and the challenges they face in an ever-changing world.

AIM (1941) As World War II threatens to draw the United States into conflict, Junior Bledsoe's cantankerous grandfather moves in, and his father dies unexpectedly. In his efforts to make sense of Pop's death, Junior makes an enemy as well as an unexpected friend, gets himself into trouble, and, with the help of his neighbors, finds his aim in life.

BLUE (1944) On the day Ann Fay Honeycutt's father goes off to war, he tells her to be the man of the house in his absence. She is keeping up with the extra responsibility fairly well until polio strikes, turning her world upside down. In the months that follow, Ann Fay faces illness, finds friendship in an unlikely place, and proves to herself just how true blue she really is.

COMFORT (1945) With Ann Fay home from the polio hospital and Daddy back from the war, life should settle into a secure rhythm. But the bombing of Hiroshima and Nagasaki awakens Daddy's war traumas. Ann Fay, who is struggling with her own disability, soon realizes she can't fix him. She summons the courage to leave home for Warm Springs, Georgia, where she finds friends, therapy, and comfort. The challenge is to bring her newfound coping skills home to her father.

DRIVE (1952) As Daddy's war trauma threatens tranquility at home, twins Ida and Ellie Honeycutt struggle to cope. Ellie escapes to the NASCAR speedway while Ida immerses herself in art. At their new high school, friendship choices drive them further apart, as does a shared attraction to a particular boy. A sudden crisis provides an opportunity to renew their deep connection and to move forward, each on her own path.

INTERVIEW WITH
JOYCE MOYER HOSTETTER

Q. How were the books in the Bakers Mountain Stories series conceived?

A. I wrote *Blue* first, after discovering a 1944 polio epidemic in my hometown's history. I knew immediately that I wanted to write this piece of human drama. Although Ann Fay Honeycutt was fictional, her experiences were things that happened to real people in the real epidemic. Like so many young people at the time, she sent her father off to war and then polio struck. Like them, Ann Fay persevered to overcome enormous challenges.

After finishing *Blue* I wanted to know more about Ann Fay's life—particularly how war would change her father and threaten their close relationship. *Comfort* deals with the aftereffects of war and polio. It is about the power of community and shared experiences to bring emotional healing.

When my publisher suggested a prequel, Ann Fay's neighbor, Junior Bledsoe, was the logical protagonist. I liked him a lot. And readers did, too. I decided to set *Aim* during 1941, the year America was drawn into the war. I wanted to explore the dynamics that shaped Junior into the steady neighbor Ann Fay had relied on in *Blue* and *Comfort*.

Drive, the story of Ann Fay's twin sisters and their struggles for personal success, is also a commemoration of local NASCAR history and a tribute to Ned Jarrett, a driver from the Bakers Mountain community.

Q. Why did you decide to write about family dysfunction?

A. A few years ago, I attended the funeral of a particularly despicable man and was startled that his eulogy made him sound like a saint. At that point, I began to dream of writing a book that opens with such a funeral and then unfolding the story to reveal the true nature of the dead man. When I began writing *Aim*, I imagined this was how I would tell Junior's story. The first scene I wrote was Pop's funeral.

However, the format and the vision changed some. In reality, Pop didn't turn out to be entirely wicked. People are complicated, and I'm convinced that every difficult adult has a wounded child hiding inside. I knew that hardship had shaped Junior's pop and also his granddaddy and his great-grandfather. Each had been battered by life. My task was to uncover enough of their lives to share their stories and to shape Junior's.

I also wanted to explore Junior's extended family and to contrast this with the steady Honeycutts. In *Blue*, the Honeycutts need Junior. But in *Aim*, he needs them. For me, this is community—giving to others when they're struggling, but also accepting help from others when we need it.

Q. How did you decide on the setting for these stories?

A. With *Blue*, I accepted a challenge to write a story from my own backyard. I grew up in the same community Ann Fay and Junior lived in. I traveled the roads they did, and I also attended Mountain View School. In my community, Bakers Mountain is an ever-present landmark.

But my family was actually from Pennsylvania. My parents moved us to North Carolina when I was one. Growing up in the south, I always felt that I lived in two worlds. My southern friends ate pimento cheese, okra, black-eyed peas, and liver mush. *My* family ate pickled beets, shoofly pie, and scrapple. But we learned to eat southern foods, too. We loved the south and the people who lived here. Except for annual visits to relatives in Pennsylvania, life in the rural south was what I knew—a landscape dotted with small farms and simple homes. Furniture factories and cotton mills were prevalent in our area. During the fifties, cotton was still grown and picked here.

I hope my readers feel my attachment to this warm and friendly place—to the rolling hills, to the rivers and creeks I played in as a child, and to the neighborliness of the families who populate my stories. I want those stories to provide a community of safety and hope for my readers.

Q. What would you like readers to know about you as an author and as a person?
A. My parents raised us on a farmstead with a creek and a pond and plenty of outbuildings for playing in. That farmstead was a shelter for me—a retreat from the larger world.

School brought me in contact with people who were sometimes cruel and with children and teachers who were different from me and my Mennonite family. I compared myself to other children, certain that I was missing out on all sorts of worldly pleasures. In my mind, other families had more money than we did, their kids had more fun, and they definitely wore more fashionable clothing. In hindsight, we were much more equal than I realized. I doubt that any of my classmates were wealthy. *My* life was rich with the things I now value most—a simple lifestyle, faith, and a large extended family that was amazingly functional.

I think I write to figure out why the world outside my sheltered life is filled with tragedy. I'll always wonder, *Why me? Why was I born into humble but safe and happy circumstances? Why is my life flooded with goodness?* I hope I never stop asking, because these questions help me to live gratefully. And perhaps they'll keep me writing, also.